CW00376565

The Advent Murder

CAT PRESTON

Copyright © 2023 Cat Preston

All rights reserved.

ISBN: 9798379106959

Chapter One

The Advent Calendar

Abby checked her reflection in the mirror making sure to smooth back the frizzy hair by her ears, before pulling on her Christmassy red, woolly hat. Pulling her coat on and adjusting her scarf, Abby turned to face the staircase. "I'm off," she shouted up the stairs. Abby waited a minute before shouting up again. "Luke?"

A door opened upstairs, and Abby heard footsteps on the landing. A head appeared over the banister. "Have fun Mum," her teenage son shouted down, an encouraging smile on his face.

Another face appeared then. "Have fun, Mrs T." The fact that her teenage son seemed to have a better love life than Abby did was not lost on her.

"Thanks guys," she replied, hoping the smile she slapped on her face covered her nervousness.

The faces disappeared, scurrying back into the privacy

of Luke's bedroom, and Abby checked the mirror one last time. Pulling on her forest green leather gloves, Abby gave herself an encouraging smile in the mirror, whispering to herself, "You've got this."

"Mum," Luke's face appeared over the banister again. "You'll be fine."

Abby looked up. "Of course I will," she said, before opening the door and feeling a blast of cold air hit her face, making her eyes water slightly. Abby jumped into her car and as soon as the engine started, put the heating on to full blast. This was it. A new adventure beckoned. Checking the mirrors to make sure she was safe to pull out, Abby took off, making her way over to Folkesdowne.

Being a bit of a loner, Abby was used to spending time by herself, but recently she'd felt a feeling she'd never really understood before: loneliness. Abby felt it all around, a feeling that her life seemed to be passing her by and she wasn't making the most of it. Her two sons had their own lives now, and Abby was struggling with the transition, more than she'd expected.

In an attempt to shake things up, Abby had volunteered to help out at the annual Living Advent Calendar event, which took place each year from the 1st to 24th December. The event was in its fourth year running, and in a bid to make a bigger impact was branching out into bigger events, which meant requiring more staff to man the events.

Tonight, 1st December, was the kick-off event. Finding the request for volunteers on social media late one night when scrolling through her phone, Abby had thought it a wonderful idea. As she jumped in the car and made her way to the meeting point, she suddenly wasn't so sure. What if everyone was too young, or too old, and it wasn't her scene? What if she didn't get on with everybody? Nerves almost got the better of her, and as Abby arrived at the location and looked for a convenient car parking spot, she wondered whether to just carry on driving and back out.

The fact that a car space opened up right in front of her made the decision for her, Abby reasoned that such luck must mean she was meant to see this through. Before she lost her nerve again, Abby forced herself out of her car and walked towards the meeting place. The street was abandoned when she reached it only minutes later, and Abby almost turned around again. She was already cold; it was dark and wet. All good reasons to go back home and snuggle into her couch with a good boxset.

Instead of turning around though, Abby waited, rubbing her hands together as she struggled to stay warm. She really hadn't thought her clothing choices through. Thinking her gloves and scarf would do the trick, Abby hadn't considered that her autumn coat was a bit too thin for the near-zero temperatures.

Abby looked up and down the street, trying to distract her mind from convincing her again that this was a bad idea. The cobblestones she stood on glimmered in the rain, reflecting light from the streetlights and moon above. Looking around, Abby could see the harbour in the distance, the little fishing boats would be languishing on the seabed now that the tide had gone out.

Realising she couldn't remember the last time she'd been out of an evening in Folkesdowne, Abby took in the night-time scenery. The tall buildings standing majestically in the rain, the glistening roads empty of the usual traffic, and the biggest thing she noticed was the quiet. The busy, little seaside town was tranquil. Abby stood in the cobbled square, closing her eyes and breathing in the salty sea air, listening to the distant sound of the water as the evening waves of the English Channel brushed against the sandy shoreline.

"Are you here for the advent thing?" A woman's voice broke the silence.

Abby turned, her eyes blinking as she focused on the advancing figure.

"I'm Lisa Lewes," the woman said, introducing herself. "Are you the only one here?"

"Looks like it," Abby said, sizing the woman up. Abby noticed immediately, and with a flicker of envy, that the woman was wearing a proper winter coat. It was a khaki-green, knee-length buttoned duvet coat, and it looked toasty. The floppy, fake fur hood seemed to frame the woman's head with a sort of halo effect. No need for a hat and scarf with that duvet-like protection, Abby thought, regretting her coat choice for the second time that night.

"Have you been waiting long?" Lisa asked, looking around.

"Not too long, 5 minutes maybe."

"Shall we walk up and see if there's any action up that way?" Lisa suggested,, pointing towards the old grain building the inaugural event was due to take place in.

Chapter Two

Door 1: The Light Show

They found the rest of the advent team keeping warm inside the old grain building, preparing for the kick-off event. With the event shrouded in mystery, with only the location of the door being revealed 48 hours prior to the event, Abby was wondering what role she would play. She thought she'd get an inkling of what would be happening, but the reveal would be as much of a surprise to her as to visitors.

There seemed to be a flurry of last minute activity as the small creative team buzzed around the building. Abby didn't know whether to wait until someone looked their way, or approach someone and offer to help. While she was trying to decide, Lisa was two steps ahead. Calling out to no-one in particular, she asked "What can we do to help?"

The buzz of the room quietened temporarily while all

attention was directed at the two middle-aged women standing at the entrance to the building. Abby squirmed and looked over to Lisa, who was smiling broadly, enjoying the attention. It was only then that Abby could see Lisa's face, without it being shrouded in shadow.

As Lisa took off her coat, she revealed a head of lush, chestnut brown, wavy hair. Her hair perfectly matched her chestnut brown eyes and olive-toned skin. Whilst she was an inch or two shorter than Abby, she had a presence about her that made her seem so much taller. A vitality. Her face shone with friendliness and warmth, like a beacon of light almost.

Jobs assigned, Abby made her way outside to greet the growing crowd of locals, keen to start the Christmas season with some fun and frivolity. In her hands was a large, red plastic tub, filled with different coloured glow sticks. Abby's job was to hand a glow stick out to each member of the audience, with an accompanying string chain to allow them to hang the glowsticks around their necks.

Lisa, meanwhile, had been drafted in to help inside, doing what Abby had no idea. Lamenting her job of standing in the freezing cold, the drizzly rain trickling down her neck, Abby felt the green monster popping in to say hello again.

A bell rang out, signalling the beginning of festivities. The big, wooden doors opened wide, beckoning people inside with Christmas music playing faintly in the background. Making sure everyone found their way inside, Abby took one last look around and almost jumped with shock as Santa appeared from the other side of the building. He brought his finger up to his lips and winked at Abby, who nodded, leaving the door slightly ajar as she went inside. Santa took up his place in the entrance, just out of sight of everyone else.

As a new song started up, everyone was told to crack their glowsticks and get ready for the show. Halfway through the song, with the hum of excited chatter in the air, the lights went out and all that could be seen was the glow from the glowsticks.

There were a lot of gasps and oohs and aahs, and even a couple of cries from a few of the younger audience members. All noise came to an end with a collective "Wow!" as suddenly bright, white snowflakes seemed to float down the walls. As the snowflakes reached the bottom of the walls, reindeers appeared against the backdrop of the main wall. They seemed to be grazing in a field, before a little bell rang again and Rudolph the Red Nosed Reindeer started playing over the speakers. A retelling of Christmas Eve preparations then began to play out in an intricate light show on the wall.

Everyone watched, mesmerised, as the reindeer were fed special food and moved into place on the sleigh. Lit up elves waved goodbye from the bottom corners of the wall as Santa appeared, walking out from the corner of the left-hand side of the wall towards the reindeers. His appearance was met by lots of gasps and excited cries of "Santa!" from the audience.

As the sleigh took off into the air, a blast of cold air blew out from above and a faint smattering of snowflakes could be felt landing. Faces raised up to the ceiling and Abby watched as little kids swiped at the snowflakes as they fell.

Abby was as mesmerised as everyone else and almost missed her cue to bring Santa inside. As the sleigh settled onto the "ground" in one of the corners of the room, Santa's famous "Ho ho ho" could be heard, and suddenly a warm white light spread across the room, and there, standing where the sleigh had come to rest, was the big man himself.

The show may have only lasted for 30 minutes but it was evident by all the smiles on the faces of the young and old as they exited the building, that the first advent had gone down a storm. The children all clutched the chocolate Santas they'd received from Santa as he'd made his way through the crowd. Everyone was already talking about what they thought would happen at tomorrow's event.

Abby stayed to help clean up all the fake snow from the floor, before heading out, her job done. It all felt a bit of an anti-climax at the end. She hadn't seen Lisa since they were given different jobs to do and the camaraderie she'd hoped to feel working as part of a team hadn't quite been there. Maybe she was expecting too much on her first day, Abby thought, although the pang of disappointment still hadn't abated by the time Abby got home.

Pouring herself a mulled wine and sticking it in the microwave to warm it up, Abby rested against the kitchen counter, feeling like her night wasn't quite finished.

Chapter Three

Door 2: The Square

Whilst Abby had approached day one of volunteering with a steady mix of excited anticipation and nervous energy, today a feeling of not quite belonging was added to the mix. Abby found she wasn't looking forward to the night as much as she had on the first night. The event itself had been amazing, but she'd felt a bit like an unnecessary, spare wheel on the volunteering front. The reality of being an ad hoc volunteer in an already established creative team hadn't matched her fantasy of it at all.

Deciding she needed a shot of positivity to get her back into the Christmas spirit, Abby gave Jane a call, listening attentively as Jane reiterated the many reasons Abby had decided to volunteer in the first place. Feeling appreciative of the opportunity to do something different and bring some Christmas cheer to local families, Abby shook off her negativity – or at least tried to – and wrapped up warm, wearing her thick, winter coat and putting her fake fur lined gloves in her bag.

Tonight, they were meeting at the local bookshop in the square for door number 2. Turning into the square, Abby was mesmerised by the twinkling lights and pretty, paper lanterns that had been strung up high, enveloping a section of the square. The bookshop looked out onto a beacon of soft light. Abby couldn't help but be impressed by the organisational skills of whoever had set this up.

Against the bookshop windows, a long table had been set up with Christmas star lights tacked to its edges. On the table sat two huge urns, along with a stack of Christmas paper cups. At the other side of the table were trays of mince pies, shortbread biscuits and chocolate digestives.

"Wow," Abby said, as the woman who had given her the role last night approached.

"Hi!" she said. "Sorry we didn't really get properly introduced last night. First night jitters and behind-the-scenes panic. I'm Hilary, one of the organisers."

Abby took Hilary's extended hand and shook it. "Last night was amazing," she said.

"Yeah, we secured lottery funding for the event this year, so we've got a bit more of a budget to do some really special doors." Hilary explained the plan for door number two and gave Abby the job of manning the snack table. Hot chocolate took up one of the urns, with the other filled with a spiced apple drink. Everyone was to be offered a hot drink and the option of either a mince pie or a couple of biscuits. The surplus supplies were hiding under the table and Abby was introduced to the runner who would be running out back for the drink refills if they happened to run out.

As Abby helped to put out some chairs, she caught a glimpse of Lisa decked out in a garish green Christmas jumper, bobbly baubles hanging off it. "Wow, I love your jumper," Abby called out.

Lisa ambled over. "Hey Abby, I missed you leaving last night."

Abby smiled apologetically. "What job are you on tonight?" she asked.

"On the door, so to speak. Meet and greet and show people to seats. I'm a glorified usher." Abby had never seen anyone so excited to be acting as an usher before. The buzz of excitable energy emanating from Lisa was intoxicating.

Wishing she had even one fifth of the positive energy Lisa seemed to have, Abby tentatively opened up a potential gap for a future friendship. "Maybe I'll see you after the event this time?" she suggested. Even hinting at a meet up on her own was a huge step for Abby, who was as much of an introvert as Lisa was an extrovert.

"Oh I would have loved to," Lisa offered her apologies. "I'm meeting a client in town after this for Christmas drinks."

"Maybe next time then?" Abby said with a smile, desperately wanting to ask Lisa what she did for a job, but not finding the nerve. The crazy thing was, if Jane and Eveline were with her, Abby wouldn't have had any issue at all with being inquisitive. She definitely needed to make it her New Year resolution to find her oomph. She was sure she'd had some at some point, she just wasn't too sure where she'd left it.

As people started arriving in the square, Abby scurried back towards the table, placing herself safely back behind the invisible barrier of helpfulness and cordiality, readying herself to play the role of host.

Asking which drink and snack people preferred was a doddle. Making small talk about the success of the previous night and everyone's excitement about what was to come, was easy. Neither required Abby to open up and put herself out there. Small talk with no expectations on either side for anything deeper was a skill Abby had mastered, to a degree. Her small talk was limited to a few choice phrases, and as Abby dealt with family after family she could hear how repetitive her conversation was. Glad when Hilary appeared on the mock stage that had been set up in front of the bookshop, Abby breathed a sigh of relief and poured herself a spiced apple drink as she settled in, leaning against the shop window, to enjoy the show.

"Tonight, boys and girls, mums and dads, and ladies and gentlemen, we have the amazing and fabulous owner of Books for all Seasons, Ron Talbert, here. He is going to read us a reimagining of one of the true Christmas classics. 'A Christmas Carol' by Charles Dickens.

Ron Talbot exited his bookshop to a round of applause, holding the picture book in his hands. A tall, red velvet wingback chair had been brought out from inside the shop, and placed in the centre of the makeshift stage. Ron walked towards the chair with his head high, looking almost regal. Taking his time to sit, he opened the book, holding it up high, cleared his voice and began.

The singsong rhythm of the writing, masterfully delivered by Ron, entranced the children sitting cross-legged at the front, where thick blankets had been laid out on the floor to protect little legs from the cold, cobblestone ground. With the picturesque setting, the deep baritone pitch of Ron's voice, and a tinkling background of soft, lilting piano music, the atmosphere was magical.

Abby breathed in the good vibes, noticing the smile of appreciation shared amongst the adults, and feeling that same emotion filling her soul. She felt a connection to everything and everyone around her in that moment, only broken by what sounded like raised voices coming from behind the square.

Chapter Four

Feeling like she should investigate given her role as helper, and not wanting the raised voices to spoil anyone else's enjoyment of the event, Abby quietly left her spot behind the table and made her way to the side of the block of shop buildings.

As she turned the corner, Abby could see movement at the end of the block. Deciding there was no other option than to take a few steps towards the action so she could tell what was going on, Abby moved closer. She was surprised to see two middle-aged men having what she could only describe as a fight, even though it looked like a pretty pitiable one. It looked like a couple of schoolkids, flailing about, kicking out with their arms and legs and shouting at each other.

Abby didn't want to get in the middle of a fight and so headed back to the corner, where she could see the event was still going on. She waved frantically in the direction of one of the male stewards. A couple of the audience members caught Abby's waving and looked around, trying to work out if the wave was directed at them.

Eventually, the steward looked up and noticed Abby. He gestured his confusion by furrowing his eyebrows and pointing his finger at his chest. Abby nodded enthusiastically, and used her own hands to gesture he should come over.

Ambling over like he didn't have a care in the world, one ear turned to the story being told, the steward approached Abby cautiously. "You wanted me?" he whispered.

"Yes," Abby replied, mirroring the whispering. "There's a fight going on around the corner."

"Oh right."

"Two middle-aged men are having some kind of half-fight, half-argument."

"Oh right. Hilarious," was all the steward could offer up.

"Maybe we can go round there, ask them to quieten down or something?" Abby suggested. Her suggestion was met with a look of horror.

"Oh no, I couldn't do that."

"I'll come with you," Abby offered.

"I've never been in a fight before," the steward protested. "What if it gets a bit violent?"

"I don't think there's any chance of that," Abby said, a flash of the scrap she had witnessed almost making her chuckle.

Abby could tell Jim, the steward, was still to be convinced about involving himself in any kind of kerfuffle. And to be fair to him, Abby had to concede that he didn't look like he came from fighting stock. But if she was going to end the fight before it disrupted the event, she needed help.

The argument was still going on when Abby and Jim made their way to the corner where Abby had been checking out the fight earlier. It had moved on now, and the bigger man seemed to be sitting on the slightly smaller man.

"See what I mean?" Abby turned to Jim, pointing at the ridiculous scene to show Jim that he had nothing to fear.

"What's going on?" Lisa suddenly appeared next to them, making them both jump.

"Look," Abby pointed out.

Lisa looked closely for a couple of minutes and then tutted. Strutting over to the two men, confidence oozing from every pore of her body, Lisa didn't stop until she was within touching distance of the men. Abby and Jim moved a little closer, not in any gallant effort to help, as Lisa looked like she could handle any situation she was confronted with. No, they moved closer purely so they could get a better look, and so they could listen in to any nuggets of wisdom she was about to impart.

"Alan?" Lisa said simply, as if she was bumping into him in a restaurant, and not when he was sitting astride another man in a back street.

Alan looked up and immediately looked sheepish. "Oh, hi Lisa," he mumbled.

"Care to explain yourself?" Lisa asked, her voice calm and casual.

"Just a little chat that got out of hand, isn't that right, Roger?"

Roger huffed some sort of reply from under Alan's coat.

"Alan, get off him!" Lisa demanded, speaking to the burly looking man as if she was in a school playground, breaking up a fight between two six year olds.

Alan begrudgingly complied, though he made sure to give Roger a kick in the groin as he got off the man.

Roger groaned, and as he turned over, his red puffed-up face came into view.

"Roger!" Lisa gasped. "What are you doing?"

Roger groaned some more, as he positioned himself into a seating position, still on the floor but looking a little more comfortable than before. "Idiot!" he muttered.

"What did you say?" Alan challenged him, taking a step closer to Roger's huddled body.

"Gentlemen, please. Is there any need for this behaviour?" Lisa berated them both.

Abby had come to the conclusion that Lisa knew both men and wondered whether it was just because they all lived close to each other, or whether there was personal history amongst them.

"Are you going to tell me what's going on?" Lisa asked, wanting to know what had caused the argument now that it was over.

Alan shrugged. "Ask him. I can't stay here in the same vicinity as that sorry excuse of a man." And with that, Alan stomped away, back in the direction of the event, which sounded like it was drawing to a conclusion too.

"We best get back," Jim said, his ears picking up the same scraping of chairs and rounds of applause that Abby had heard.

As Jim headed back, considering his job done, Abby asked, "Do you want me to stay?"

Lisa looked over, having forgotten for a moment that they'd had an audience.

"We're good here. I might stay with Roger for a bit and make sure he's okay. Thanks Abby."

Abby headed back to help with the clear up. People

had already started leaving when she turned back into the square.

Chapter Five

Door 3: A Christmas Story

When Abby got home, she called Jane and told her all about her action-filled night. Of course, Jane and Eveline had a thousand and one questions, all of which remained unanswered. Abby had hung around for as long as she could after clearing up, hoping Lisa would re-appear and explain what had happened, but she must have left with Roger, whoever he was.

With strict instructions to update Jane as soon as she was home from the next night's event, Abby went to bed. Sleep eluded her though, as anticipation about the next day mixed with the energy she'd felt this night, being embroiled in drama. Except for her adventures with Jane and Eveline, this was the first time in longer than she could remember that Abby felt a frisson of excitement when reflecting on her day.

The next morning, Abby felt groggy and irritable as the lack of sleep punished her. She was three coffees in before she even felt like a human again.

Abby had promised to head out early with Luke to get him new shoes but it wasn't until 11am that they left the house. With their first stop being a café so Abby could top up with more coffee, she managed to make it around the shopping centre and get home with enough time to have a nap before the next event.

She spent the whole drive over to Folkesdowne wondering if Lisa would be there, but when she arrived at the library, which was opening late especially for the event, she didn't see Lisa anywhere.

Trying to hide her disappointment, Abby walked straight over to Hilary. Tonight's event was a retelling of Christmas across the Years, and Abby's role for the night was as a steward again. She was discovering that volunteering at an event like this was basically just standing around, enjoying the show. All the hard work was done by the organisers and the creative team.

Abby had already decided that the point of her being there was solely as a hi-viz jacket wearer, an information point for any audience member who needed help or directions. Not that she was complaining. Abby was only just into day three and she was starting to feel like she was part of something special. Thinking about it, the hi-viz made her feel quite important. Abby wondered whether she should buy one for everyday use.

The event was not what Abby had expected at all. A researcher from the library gave a fascinating talk on the early origins of Christmas. Top of the list was how things we celebrate now can be traced back to the pagans, who held festivals based around the Wheel of the Year.

A big part of the pagan festivities was celebrating Yule, and the Winter Solstice. When paganism was practiced, one of the many traditions involved finding a log, often from an oak or birch tree and usually one found lying on the ground in woodland. People would decorate it with cuttings of evergreen or holly and ivy. Eight holes were bored into the log and candles placed in each hole to be lit on the night of the winter solstice. The log was then burned, though a piece of it was saved to kindle the fire of the next year.

Abby had known that the Christmas tree had been introduced in Germany in the 17th century, and had become popular in England with Queen Charlotte first introducing it in 1800. Prince Albert, Queen Victoria's consort, was credited as being the one who made it popular with the masses.

Finding out that pagan stories of old spirits travelling through the sky in midwinter was one of the origin stories for Father Christmas was a surprise though. As was the revelation that celebrating Christmas as the birth of Jesus wasn't introduced until the 4th century. In early Christianity, Jesus's birthday wasn't something that was initially celebrated.

When the researcher shared that Christmas was cancelled in England in the days of Oliver Cromwell, a chorus of boos rose up from the children sitting on the floor in front of the young man giving the talk.

Abby had nothing but admiration for the man. He had somehow managed to captivate the attention of the children while also holding the interest of the adults with his fascinating facts. Abby even made a note to herself to check if the library did a more detailed talk on the same subject as she was loving the mini history lesson.

She could have listened to the stories of how we came

to celebrate Christmas all evening and was sorry when the talk came to an end. An invitation was given to all the children to head to the children's room in the library, where craft tables had been laid out with Christmas colouring pages and lollipop sticks and string to make Christmas stars.

With the children amused, the adults were invited to have a wander around the library, able to use their library cards to take home a few books. Realising she hadn't stepped foot in a library in years, since her boys were small, Abby searched in her purse. She found her old library card hiding behind one of her store points cards. Her duties for the night complete, Abby took the opportunity to browse amongst the folklore section of British history.

Coming away with 2 pagan history books, Abby couldn't help taking a peek in the cosy mystery section, adding to her hoard. If nothing else happened in the month of December, at last she had some company in the form of all the books she'd picked up, Abby thought as she headed back to her car. Day 3 done, and Abby felt like she'd had 3 completely different experiences.

Chapter Six

Door 4: Opera

She felt a pang of disappointment that she'd be missing day 4's door, due to a school event, and was almost tempted to forgo the school's Christmas concert. As it turned out though, Abby would have missed her son, Luke, giving an impromptu performance as Rosencrantz, in a Christmas-themed performance of Hamlet.

The performance was a peculiar mash up with Dickens's A Christmas Carol. Hamlet's father was, of course, the ghost of Christmas past, with Ophelia playing the Ghost of Christmas yet to come and Horatio playing the Ghost of Christmas Present.

It was maybe the strangest, yet most imaginative, Christmas play Abby had ever seen. To witness her son, who she would never have imagined as having the confidence to stand up on stage in front of such a big audience, brimming with life and standing tall and proud, Abby felt her throat constricting and her eyes tearing up.

She'd never been prouder of Luke, and had to stop herself from harassing the strangers sitting next to her, to point out her connection to the young man on stage speaking so eloquently. If only she had someone here with her who could share in her joy, that one other person who could feel that same immense feeling of pride and overwhelming love.

Seeing her son up on stage made Abby think of her eldest son, Will, who was up in Liverpool, studying medicine at the University of Liverpool. She couldn't wait to see him again. Even though she only saw him in October, to Abby it felt like half a lifetime ago. Going from being completely all over and on top of both of her boys schedules, to being a spectator on the sidelines, was hard to get used to at any time of the year, but especially at Christmas.

Christmas was always a magical time of year for Abby. Not caring much for shopping, unless it meant strolling up and down a small town high street with lots of local stores, it was the other things that made Christmas special for Abby. Taking the boys to pick a Christmas tree at a local farm, and decorating it together with hot chocolates in hand, the boys fighting about who got to put what decoration where.

It was all the traditions that Abby loved, and creating memories out of honouring those traditions, made the fact that the boys now wanted to create their own memories with their friends was the bit that Abby struggled with the most. Maybe that was why she'd really signed up for the advent calendar event. Maybe getting to share in the magic of each day's door somehow filled a gap left by all the traditions she now found abandoned in favour of nights out with friends, and nights in with girlfriends.

Chapter Seven

Door 5: The Bandstand

Abby found herself rushing to get ready for day 5's advent door. She'd watched day 4's video which they posted on their social media groups. The event had been an operatic performance by a local opera group. Not having been to an opera before, Abby wasn't sure whether to be upset she'd missed it or relieved. She wondered whether she should add going to an opera to her bucket list of things to do before she was 50, as she headed out the door for day 5's event.

All Abby knew about tonight was that it was an outdoor event at the bandstand, located just off the high street, and near the park. To Abby, this could only mean one thing: a winter coat and woolly hat were definitely required.

Again, Abby's job was to encourage people to congregate in the designated areas. She had even been given a special 5-foot light so people could find help easily if needed. The light was even more impressive than the hi-viz jacket, Abby had decided, holding it proudly to her left side like a wizard's staff, as she welcomed visitors.

Some chairs had been set up near the front of the bandstand for anyone finding it difficult to stand, but most people were happy standing, some stomping their feet to keep warm. Abby kept her eye out for Lisa, but there was no sign of her.

With the event due to start any minute, Abby found herself in a position on the edge of the audience, ready to move people towards the exit path at the end. Without realising, she'd picked one of the prime spots. If she looked past the bandstand, she could see the group of singers gathered on the other side, adjusting their choir outfits and chatting animatedly with each other. She watched as a hush fell over them as their choirmaster raised her hand above her head, holding all 5 fingers up before counting down silently by folding each finger down for each second countdown. When her hand had been shaped into a fist, a woman at the front of the queue they'd formed started singing "We Wish You a Merry Christmas".

The solitary singer walked up the steps on the side of the bandstand the audience couldn't see, appearing in the middle of the circular stage as she sang the word "Christmas". As she got to the 3rd iteration of "We Wish You a Merry Christmas" the other choir members appeared from behind the woman. All of the choir joined in on the line "And a Happy New Year". As the remainder of the song played out, the choir arranged itself into 2 semicircles, all 30 faces looking out at the crowd.

Four songs in, Abby noticed one of the female members of the crowd looking distractedly to the side of her. Abby tried to work out what was distracting her, but part of the bandstand was blocking her view.

With Abby's attention shared between the crowd directly in front of her and the choir performing in the bandstand, Abby almost missed it when the same woman disappeared from the front row of the semicircle and started moving to the back of the group. And then suddenly, she was off, running down the steps out the back, towards whatever it was that had drawn her attention earlier.

Abby wondered whether she should go and see whether the woman needed any help, but really, what could she possibly do if she did? Reflecting on what had happened only 3 days earlier, Abby found herself wishing Lisa was here. She barely knew the woman, and yet she had a feeling Lisa wouldn't have questioned what to do, she'd have jumped into action and be halfway around the bandstand by now.

What to do with the light post though? Leave it resting on the lamppost beside her? But then what if it caused a health and safety issue? Should she take it with her? But then wouldn't that just attract everyone else's attention? Still dithering, but with no idea what was happening behind the bandstand, all Abby knew was that the woman hadn't come back.

Asking herself the only question Abby could think was left – what if something horrific was happening and she was standing here doing nothing? – Abby found her feet and made the decision for her, taking her off in the direction of the back of the bandstand.

Out of the corner of her eye, Abby spotted Jim, and made a slight detour to transfer custody of the light post, meaning she could now quicken her pace without drawing attention to herself.

Turning the corner onto the tree-lined pathway that led away from the bandstand, Abby had to stop and wait for a few seconds while her eyes adjusted to the change in lighting, with the lights around the front of the bandstand not stretching all the way around to the back. Frosty darkness took over, sending everything into the shadows.

Abby heard the noise before she could make out who was making it. She heard raised voices, but couldn't make out how many voices she heard. Walking forward, she hesitated, realising she was about to walk into a dark, shadowy expanse of parkland. The area wasn't known for being dangerous, and she knew there were about 50 people just one scream away, but instinct and the ingrained sense of danger made her hesitate all the same.

It was the woman's cry that steered her forward, a bravery she didn't know she had suddenly filling her up and pushing her on, all her senses now on high alert. Abby had no idea what to expect, but the sight she was met with flushed away any panic she'd felt.

Her fear was replaced by a mixture of annoyance and amusement, as Abby moved forward. "Roger?" she called out, announcing her presence to the 3 people currently in some form of stand-off. The woman was sandwiched between Roger, the man from the fight Abby had intervened in just the other day, and another man Abby didn't recognise.

"Are you okay?" she asked. Directing her question to the woman, but without knowing her name, leaving it ambiguous.

"Oh, hi Abby," Roger said sheepishly, rewarding her with a meek wave.

"What's going on?" Abby asked. "Should I maybe call

someone over?"

"I've got this," the woman said, her voice edgy, with a hint of frustration.

"Just having a chat with Roxie and her fiancé," Roger explained, seemingly enjoying the predicament. "Abby, meet Lance."

Lance did not look pleased to see either Abby or Roger. "You better get me away from this man," Lance snarled at Roxie.

Roxie looked over at Abby. "Can you let Sue, the choirmaster, know I had to dash off?"

"Erm, sure," Abby said, wondering what she'd walked in on. She couldn't help but watch, fascinated at everything being communicated by body language, as Roxie tried to pull Lance away.

"Call me," Roger called after Roxie, laughing as Lance tried to break away from Roxie's grip.

He wasn't so cavalier when Roxie let go though, yelping as he jumped into the air and ran towards, and then past, Abby as Lance advanced.

"That's right, run, you little weasel," Lance shouted after Roger's disappearing figure.

Abby had to step to the side as Lance came barrelling towards her, pulling up almost nose to nose with Abby.

Lance was breathing heavily, Abby could feel the anger emanating from him and took an instinctive step back.

"Sorry," Lance muttered, turning away and walking quickly back towards Roxie, who was waiting on the path, hands on her hips.

As they moved away, Abby heard Roxie ask Lance: "What would you have done if you'd caught him?"

Abby had to wonder about some people. As she turned and walked back towards the friendlier side of the bandstand Abby wondered who this Roger was. Day 5 and she'd already caught him in 2 different fights, with 2 different men. Who was this Roger? And why on earth was he hanging around the advent events, picking fights with other men?

What was weirder, Abby thought, is that he looked like the least likely fighter Abby had ever met. His whole demeanour had more of a 'lover' vibe about it. Maybe that was the problem, Abby wondered, chuckling to herself.

Getting back to her position just in time to see the last song, Abby's heart wasn't really in the event anymore. She couldn't help but wonder about who Roger was, and what he was embroiled in.

It was only as a local children's choir took to the stage to help the adults with their version of John Lennon's Happy Christmas (War is Over) did Abby feel a little bit of Christmas joy rekindle inside, pushing her thoughts of Roger out of the way. By the time Abby got home though, all she could think about was Roger and his fighting.

Chapter Eight

Door 6, 7 and 8

Recounting the story to Eveline and Jane over the phone that night, Abby wondered whether Roger would be a regular distraction at future advent events. "I just don't understand where he comes into it all," Abby said, intrigued.

"But you said Lisa knew him? You know small towns Abby, maybe it all seems so weird to you because this isn't your small town?" Eveline suggested.

"True," Jane added. "And maybe in that small town, he is a known character?"

"I guess," Abby conceded.

"He sounds like the town's local cad to me," Eveline said, amused at the idea of a man roaming around entrancing the women of the town into affairs of the heart.

"I wonder if he's a bachelor?" Jane said, wanting to know his history. "You should try and find out his story, Abby. Everyone has a story by the time you get to 40. Either he's been hurt in love, unlucky in love or doesn't really know how to do love."

"And there'll be a backstory for each one of those scenarios too," Eveline said. "The human condition is so fascinating."

"What's tomorrow's day then? I wonder if there'll be any action there." Jane said.

"I wonder whether Lisa will be there again?" Eveline added.

"You know, it's almost like you two are part of this adventure of mine. You both know as much about it as I do," Abby noted.

Jane laughed. "Well, if there's any more adventure in this advent business, we might have to come and gate-crash. What do you say, Eveline?"

"Oh, absolutely!" Eveline agreed. Abby could almost hear the enthusiastic nodding over the phone. "Maybe we should come down for some Christmas shopping?"

"And maybe some Roger the Dodger action?" Jane added, chuckling.

"Roger the Dodger!?" Abby said.

"Who's that dodging the ladies and dodging the fights," Jane sang.

"It's Roger the Dodger, ooh yeah, that's right." Eveline finished off.

They both started laughing hysterically at their made up rhyme, causing Abby to hold the phone away from her ear to stop the cackling from leaving any permanent damage to her eardrum.

The next few days went without a hitch, and without a sighting of Lisa or Roger. Abby hoped it wasn't the last she'd see of Lisa, but she would be quite happy if she didn't have to deal with Roger again.

Day 6 had been outside a local church. The church band put on a performance. Then there was a beautiful retelling of the birth of Jesus Christ told by the resident priest, with the help of some of the Sunday school children.

Day 7 was the local circus school, who performed juggling acts and taught children how to juggle and tightrope walks and do some simple tricks. Abby hadn't even known there was a local circus school, marvelling at the breadth of choices available locally for kids in the area. She didn't remember anything as exotic back in the days of her own childhood.

Abby did remember doing karate for a few months when she was younger. She remembered enjoying those lessons until it came time to do some one-on-one combat practice, at which point she gave it up for fear of getting hurt. The local martial arts group, who hosted Day 8's door, reminded Abby of her youth. When they invited the audience to come onto the mat and try some of the basic routines, Abby made sure to step as far back as she could. Watching a performance from the sidelines was enjoyable, having to participate in the performance was something else entirely.

Chapter Nine

Door 9: The Railway

By day 9, Abby found herself in a routine. She'd attend the event, which usually started at 6pm, and then head home and cook tea for herself and Luke. They'd sit on the couch eating together, while watching one of their shows, which usually involved a murder and a tormented detective.

The location for day 9's door was the steam railway station, who were giving guests a quick ride up and down the track on one of their steam engines. The event was definitely one of the highlights of the advent calendar, and the audience had shown up en masse for the event. This meant that Abby was on duty from the moment she arrived.

As soon as Hilary had given her the brief, she'd had one of the floor-length torches thrust into her hands and had been directed out to the front entrance for crowd control. Throngs of excited families were waiting to be allowed through the doors, to the train beyond. Abby's job was to keep them entertained for the next 20 minutes while some last minute preparations were made.

The idea of entertaining anyone made Abby want to break out in hives. Shuffling out of the side entrance, Abby made her way to the front of the growing crowd, nervously practicing her small talk as she made her way along the queue. Once at the front, Abby cast an enthusiastic smile out into the audience and called out a couple of "Not long now!", feeling very socially awkward. The relief flooded over her as she saw Lisa approaching.

"Hey stranger," Lisa said smiling as she joined Abby at the front of the queue. "Riling up the crowd?"

"I am so glad you're here!" Abby whispered, thankful for the company, and of being able to offload the duties of keeping the crowd entertained.

Lisa smiled warmly, making Abby feel like she was seen, heard and understood all in one single gesture. Lisa turned to the crowd, "How are we all doing tonight?" she called out, as if a compere at a theatre.

The crowd cheered and shouted their responses back, connecting immediately.

"Looking forward to a magical ride on a mystical steam train?" Lisa shouted, to a resounding cheer.

As the doors opened and the crowd moved through the shop and out onto the platform, Abby and Lisa moved with them. Their next jobs were to help direct people onto the train compartments, making sure everyone got a seat before the train blew its steam horn to mark its departure. The journey was only a short one, a taste of what it was like to ride an old steam engine, for those that hadn't done it before, and an invitation to join them on the steam railway's own Christmas events.

The ride took people up to the next station and back. Along the short route, wooden reindeers had been stationed and railway volunteers were dressed up in elf costumes, waving at the families as they passed by.

Rain had threatened but the evening turned out perfectly, a brisk coastal wind blew in and the moon shone brightly up in the sky, lighting up the fields on either side of the track. Santa Claus made an appearance, passing through the train and giving each child a chocolate bar or lollypop. Santa was followed up by a railway employee, who had a little trolley, offering the option of hot chocolates or tea and coffee.

Abby was waiting back at the station when the train pulled back in, ready to hand out little goody bags with railway stickers inside, a leaflet of upcoming events and a discount token for the remaining Santa Specials. If she'd have thought the buzz of excitement boarding the train was high, the atmosphere when people started to disembark was even more electric. It seemed that children never tired of seeing Santa, each time being just as magical as the last.

"That was so much fun," Lisa said, appearing by Abby's side as Abby said goodnight to some of the stragglers.

"It was brilliant. I can't believe there's so many different doors happening. It's completely different each night."

"I wish they'd done stuff like this when we were little," Lisa said, a big grin on her face. "So, do you have to shoot off tonight, or do you fancy that drink?"

Abby hesitated, anxious about taking the next step to

possibly acquiring a new friend, but before she could decide how to answer they were interrupted by a scream that sounded like it came from the back of the railway station.

Abby and Lisa ran around back to see what was happening, both reacting instinctively. They stopped short as they neared the back of the station though, as it was bathed in darkness and shadows. It was only the second scream that pushed them forward, and that was when Abby almost bumped into a woman, standing by one of the tall bins, her hand clamped to her mouth.

Chapter Ten

As Abby stepped closer to the woman, she saw what had made her cry out. A body lay slumped face down on the floor, immobile.

Lisa followed Abby's gaze. "Oh my..." she cried, almost losing her footing, and having to grab at the cold, brick wall to keep herself upright.

Seeing the shock on Lisa's face and noticing the woman who'd screamed slump to the ground, edging closer to the body, reaching out, trying to touch it, Abby knew she had to take control. She reached for the woman, pulling her back, but not quick enough to stop her from touching the hair of the man who was lying face down.

From all the movement around her, Abby hadn't seen the man move. She'd seen enough police dramas, and had even attended a few crime scenes herself, to know the importance of maintaining the scene, but she also realized that she'd have to check the man's vitals, to determine whether he was still alive or not.

As more people from the advent group and railway staff made their way towards them, Abby held up her hand. "Stop," she said. "Someone call the police, and maybe the ambulance." She leant down to see if she could notice any breathing, simultaneously holding her fingertips to the man's wrist and then neck to check if she could find a pulse. There was no movement. Leaning back, resting on her feet in a squat position, she made eye contact with the man who was on the phone to the emergency services, and slowly shrugged her shoulders, indicating she wasn't sure whether the man was breathing or not.

The man edged forwards, receiving instructions from the 999 operator on what to do until the ambulance arrived and could take over.

Abby heard a gasp to her right and looked over as Lisa started crying, covering her mouth with her hand, trying to stay quiet. The woman who had found the body sat on the floor, rocking back and forth. Abby moved closer to her, worried she might be experiencing shock.

As the man performed CPR, someone inside the building must have turned on the external lights as they were suddenly flooded with harsh light.

Abby noticed blood on the woman's hands, smeared across her palm, and looked back at the body to see whether she could tell where the blood had come from. The lights had made the man's face clearly visible, and Abby gasped as the realization of who she was looking at dawned on her.

"Police and ambulance are on their way," the man who was giving CPR said. Another man came over to give the first one a break from the exhausting work of trying to keep a man's heart pumping.

Abby looked around at the scene. She knew it was important to keep a scene as secure as possible and have everything as undisturbed as could be.

The woman stood up abruptly. "I've got to get out of here," she said.

"No!" Abby warned her. "You have to stay where you are. The police will need to question you, you can't go anywhere until they release you."

"I don't care," the woman said. "I can't be here."

"Wait, please." Abby realized she didn't know the woman's name. "Sorry," she said, trying to distract the woman from leaving. "I don't even know your name."

The woman blinked, her brain registering the normalcy of the question in the midst of the fog of everything else. She looked at Abby. "It's Marjory," she said, her voice low.

Abby tried to smile, attempting to keep up the charade of normalcy. "I'm Abby," she introduced herself.

The noise of a siren appeared then, heralding the arrival of the first emergency services vehicle. Abby felt her whole body sigh, a release of tension as a police car rolled into the station, an ambulance directly on its heels.

An ambulance woman rushed out of the vehicle, heading over to the body, while the other grabbed the kit and followed behind. Despite trying to revive the man, he was declared dead at the scene. The two men that had been doing CPR collapsed on a nearby wall, exhausted and distraught.

Abby looked around, feeling overwhelmed. With the ambulance staff focused on the body, Abby looked from Lisa, who was now collapsed on the floor, to Marjory, and back to the two men who had stopped performing CPR, visibly shaken and exhausted. Relieved to see a policewoman approaching Marjory, Abby felt her own knees start to wobble, and had to reach out her hand to steady herself.

An unmarked car arrived on the scene, pulling in behind the police car. A woman jumped out of the car and strode confidently towards the crime scene. Two police officers from the police car fell into line behind her, making Abby wonder if the woman was in charge. In all her dealings with the police so far, Abby had yet to meet a senior female police officer, so wasn't too sure what to expect.

"Can someone tell me what happened here?" the woman asked, introducing herself as DS Murphy.

All eyes turned to Abby and she stood, giving her name and the reason why she, and everyone else, was here. "We were just closing up, and myself and Lisa," Abby pointed to Lisa, who was still sitting against the wall. Noting that Lisa had now stopped crying, Abby wasn't sure whether that was a good thing or not, as instead Lisa was sitting staring vacantly out. Abby waited a second to see if Lisa would acknowledge her story, but when she didn't, Abby carried on. "We heard a scream from just inside the building, and we ran out."

"The scream came from inside the building?" DS Murphy asked.

"Sorry, no. The scream came from out here somewhere, we were inside when we heard it," Abby corrected herself.

While Abby recanted the rest of the events leading up to the police arriving, DS Murphy walked over to the body to check and confirmed with the ambulance woman that they were now dealing with a dead body. She made a sign to one of the officers, who then turned, heading back to the police car.

DS Murphy stood up from kneeling beside the body

and pulled out a notebook. "Okay, I'm going to have to ask you all to stop any and all conversations, stand apart from each other please. Constable Ryan will take each of your details and a preliminary statement, and then you will be allowed to go home. I know this is very distressing and we appreciate your help."

Abby wiped her hand across her face, feeling exhausted suddenly.

"Who was the first to find the body?" DS Murphy asked.

Abby pointed to Marjory, who had frozen on the spot at the sight of the police.

As Constable Ryan made his way over to the railway volunteers to take their statements, the other officer re-appeared from his car carrying crime scene tape.

DS Murphy took some details from Marjory, finishing up just as another police car pulled into the car park. Rather than approach the deceased body, DS Murphy directed the police officers to Marjory. Abby caught Murphy's eye and pointed towards Lisa, who was now rocking back and forth. One of the ambulance personnel was asked to check her vitals and assess her condition.

As the scene started to fill up with more police cars, Abby was handed a cup of tea by one of the railway volunteers who had been inside the building and had not exited until after the emergency services had turned up, wondering what was happening. After giving everyone a drink and getting the lowdown from more than one witness, the man was sent home. The detectives were now arriving, starting to take preliminary witness statements from the other witnesses.

Abby watched from the corner of her eye as a van marked "Coroner" pulled in, followed closely by a Forensics van.

DS Murphy was scrupulous in her note-taking, making Abby walk through every second she could remember, including where she saw Marjory standing and the positions of everyone else in the yard once the discovery had been made. Abby made sure to tell Murphy about pulling Marjory away from the body, and the bloody mark she saw on Marjory's palm from where she must have touched the head wound.

It was over 2 hours before Abby was released. Her head was pounding at this point and all she wanted to do was crawl into bed and sleep for a week. She wondered how Lisa was, not having spoken to her since the police arrived. The whole night was quickly turning into a blur as Abby felt her body starting to shut down.

"Is there anyone at home?" DS Murphy asked.

"Just my son." Abby said. "He'll be wondering where I am."

"Did you drive here?" DS Murphy was wondering whether she should allow Abby to drive home or not. She'd noticed Abby becoming a little unstable on her feet as the events of the night were starting to catch up with her and decided to ask one of the police officers to drive Abby home. "Will your son be home?"

"Yes," said Abby.

"Okay then, Constable Ryan here will drive you home. You can come and collect your car tomorrow, okay? And I'll be in touch if I have any more questions."

Abby didn't have the energy to argue. While a little voice inside warned Abby that coming to get her car the next day would be a nuisance, she chose to ignore it as she let her head rest against the seat headrest, closing her eyes and trying to rid herself of the image of Roger's face staring vacantly up at her.

Chapter Eleven

Luke opened the door as soon as he saw the police car making its way slowly down the road. Abby had been allowed to call home to let Luke know why she was so late in case he'd started worrying. From the look on his face, it hadn't quite worked.

He'd known straightaway that something was wrong when his mum had called, overhearing a policeman in the background talking on his two-way radio. Abby had tried to make light of her situation and blame it on the event overrunning, but Luke could hear the worry in her voice.

As Abby walked through the front door, Luke embraced her in a bear hug. "You okay, Mum?" he asked, concerned.

"I'll be okay, kiddo. Just a bit of a shock to the system."

"You should be getting used to finding dead bodies by now." Luke said, trying to lighten the mood.

Abby mustered up enough energy to smile and squeeze Luke's hand, before heading for the stairs. "I'm shattered, do you mind if I go straight up?"

"Sure," Luke said, suddenly sounding very grown up.

"I'll bring you up one of your night-time teas and lock up, okay?"

Abby couldn't love him more than she did in that moment. Sometimes, being a single mum, she felt like she missed out on having that special someone to lean on and look after her in her times of need, and here was her teenage son doing just that. "Love you loads," she said, blowing Luke a kiss as she headed upstairs.

By the time Luke had locked up and made the tea, Abby was out for the count. She hadn't even bothered taking off her make up, it all just felt too much like hard work.

Luke tucked his mum in and kissed her softly on the forehead. He left the tea on her bedside table just in case she woke up, and then tiptoed out of the room.

It was midday before Abby stirred the next day. Grabbing her dressing gown, she slowly headed downstairs to grab herself a cup of tea. Luke was there, waiting for her to wake up.

"Hey Mum, how are you feeling this morning?" He'd been so concerned he'd stayed off school, and sat waiting for her, to make sure she was feeling better.

Abby didn't know whether to be mad that he'd skipped school or proud of him for being so caring. The caring won though, because how could she not love that he wanted to make sure she was okay.

"I called Will. He said to call and let him know you're okay. He told me to tell you he could come home early if you want?"

Abby wondered whether this was the point that the roles became reversed, and they moved into the adulting roles? She definitely wasn't ready for that, not yet anyway, maybe not ever?

"I'm feeling much better today." Abby reassured her

son. "And thank you so much for looking after me last night. I really appreciate it."

Luke smiled, feeling embarrassed, but also a little bit proud that he was there when his mum needed him to be.

"I hope you look after me like that when I'm old and decrepit," Abby said, teasing.

"That'll be Will's job," Luke said. "He's the oldest."

Abby laughed. The phone in the hallway interrupted any further conversation. "Uh oh," Abby said. "I wonder who that's going to be."

Luke went out into the hallway to grab the house phone, sheepishly coming back in seconds later. "I might have also called Jane and Eveline last night," he said, passing the phone to Abby.

As Abby looked at the number on the front of the phone screen, Luke grabbed his tea and made a beeline for his room. Now that he'd made sure his mum was okay, it was time he headed into school, if he was quick he could make it just as lunch finished.

"Hey," Abby said, holding the phone up to her ear. "I'm fine."

"Oh, good to hear," Eveline's voice echoed down the phone line.

"When did Luke call you? And what did he tell you?" Abby asked, wondering whether Luke had sent out a distress signal or not.

"That you've gone and got yourself into another fine mess," Eveline said.

"Charming!" Abby retorted.

There was a crackling noise over the phone, followed by a short moment of silence before Jane's voice came booming out.

"How's Luke?" asked Jane. "Poor thing was worried sick about you."

"He's good now. He was a godsend last night though, was a perfect little gentleman."

"Good to hear. You've raised him well." Jane said. "And how are you?"

"I'm fine now. Yesterday evening just took it out of me. Completely not what I expected at all."

"Well, I bet!" Jane said. "Listen, we've got no plans this week, and what with you getting yourself involved in another murder investigation and all, we wondered, do you want company?"

Abby opened her mouth to reply, but before she could Jane soldiered on.

"Feel free to say no, and we'll say no more about it. But if you do, well we can be there by teatime, maybe slightly later, like wine o'clock?"

Abby hesitated. She loved having Jane and Eveline stay, but she'd been feeling really proud of herself for getting involved in the community advent on her own, putting herself out there and meeting new people. Part of her wanted to thank them for the offer and politely decline. But another part of her knew that having a good group of friends who would drop everything to come and cheer you up was priceless, and not to be squandered.

"I'll get the wine in then?" Abby asked.

"Fab. See you later, dear." Jane said, hanging up.

Chapter Twelve

Door 10: Cancelled

The knock on the door signalled the arrival of Eveline and Jane, or so Abby thought. But it wasn't them, meaning Abby was a bit taken aback to find Lisa standing at her door.

Abby's first thought was how on earth had Lisa found her home, but then she remembered texting her address to Lisa just that afternoon. "Sorry," Abby said, finally opening the door wide after leaving Lisa standing awkwardly on the front step while her brain played catch up.

As Lisa followed Abby through to her kitchen, Abby apologised again for completely forgetting she'd given Lisa an open invite.

"I'm sorry I just turned up like this," Lisa said, as she made her way into Abby's kitchen. "My head is a mess. I just can't get the image out of my mind. I know you saw the same thing."

"You thought we could be horrified together rather than alone?" Abby asked, with a wry smile.

"Kind of," Lisa said, a nervous laugh escaping from her throat.

Abby offered Lisa a seat at the kitchen island and Lisa took the décor in as Abby turned to put the kettle on.

"I love what you've done with this room," Lisa said. "It's so cosy, in a good way, not in a small way, obviously."

Abby turned and smiled. "Thank you, it's my favourite room in the house."

"Did it used to be…" Lisa's voice trailed off as she noticed the unusual features in the room.

"Two rooms instead of one?" Abby finished off Lisa's question.

Lisa nodded.

"It did. The house used to be two separate fishing cottages. They were knocked together years ago to form one bigger house. So, this space here used to be two separate kitchens." Abby looked around her kitchen for the millionth time. Each time she did, she seemed to appreciate it even more.

She'd installed a new kitchen a few years ago, which had been the exact kitchen she'd been picturing in her head for years. A kitchen island took pride of place in the middle of the big room, which also had an extension to the side, which had been fitted out as a snug. A soft pink loveseat was set snuggly against the wall, a tv hanging on the wall opposite so the boys could sit in the room and watch tv while Abby cooked.

In the daytime, Abby seemed to live in the kitchen. She sat at the island to do her work, always close to the kettle. Most of her entertaining was done in the kitchen too, and it wasn't until the evening that she'd retreat to the living room and snuggle down in her favourite oversized chair and watch tv or read.

"You seemed to handle yesterday so much better than I did," Lisa said.

"I might have had a bit of recent exposure to death," Abby confessed, wondering how to explain her crazy adventures of the last year.

"Oh, I'm so sorry," Lisa said, her face twisted in regret.

"No no, nothing painful. Sorry, I probably should have explained a bit better."

Not knowing how to tell her story, Abby felt a wave of relief as she was saved by the doorbell. Before she could get up to answer the door though, she heard footsteps running down the stairs.

"I'll get it," Luke called out.

Abby heard a flurry of welcomes before the door to the kitchen was flung open and a purple-haired Jane pranced through the doorway. Arms opening wide, Jane advanced on Abby like a carnivore moving in on its prey.

"Abby dear," Jane said, wrapping her arms tightly around Abby's body. As she pulled her arms away, Jane deposited a kiss on each of Abby's cheeks. "How are you doing?" Grabbing Abby's face and looking steadily into her eyes, Abby felt almost as if she was getting a full medical by the power of a gaze.

Eveline appeared then. "Unhand the woman, Jane." Pushing Jane out of the way, Eveline leaned in and pecked Abby lightly on the cheek. "You are an absolute embarrassment sometimes," Eveline said, turning back to Jane to rebuke her.

Jane ignored Eveline, noticing Lisa sitting at the table, and moved in her direction to dole out another of her overly affectionate greetings.

"I'm Jane, dear. I assume Abby must have told you all about us?" Jane fluffed up her hair and stood back, almost as if she was presenting herself to Lisa.

Lisa's eyes darted over to Abby, wondering who this ebullient woman was.

"We've been here twice Jane," Eveline said, before Abby had a chance to interject. "Honestly, the woman thinks she's famous around these parts or something."

"Well, we have solved two murders while here, haven't we?" Jane argued.

"You have?" Lisa asked, incredulous. She looked over at Abby, who had a guilty look on her face.

Before the conversation got any more absurd, Abby decided she better make some proper introductions. "Lisa, these are my good friends from Yorkshire. Eveline here used to be in the Yorkshire police force but is obviously now retired."

"Less of the obviously, thank you very much." Eveline interrupted, stepping forward and shaking Lisa's hand. "I'm the cool, calm, collected one."

"What does that make me?" Jane piped up.

"The lovely, lively, chatty one," Abby said, avoiding the scornful look she was sure Eveline was directing her way.

"So, how do you all know each other?" Lisa asked.

"We met in Menorca," Abby explained. "On holiday."

"And we solved a couple of murders together too," Jane added.

"Jane!" Abby shot Jane a warning glance. The last thing she wanted to do was scare Lisa away, and she was already picking up on some confusing vibes emanating from the stool Lisa was perching on.

"Three murders," Eveline corrected.

"You don't need to join in, Eveline." Abby said, feeling herself getting more and more flustered.

"So, let me get this straight," Lisa said, staggered at what she was hearing. "You all met in Menorca, solved three murders, and then came back to the UK and solved two more?"

"Pretty much," Jane said, nodding proudly.

"Yup," Eveline added.

Abby groaned. This was not the first impression she was looking to create.

"Abby, who are you?" Lisa asked, wondering how this timid looking woman could be any part of a murder-solving group.

Abby squirmed on her seat. "I'm just normal, like you."

"Oh you're anything but normal, Abby dear." Jane corrected her, smiling affectionately at Abby as she paid her what she considered to be an amazing compliment.

But Abby didn't want any accolades, and she certainly didn't want to be called out as different in any way. Abby liked it best when she flew under the radar, hiding just beneath the surface. The problem, she realized, was that she had gone and made friends with people who had no idea what it meant to fly under the radar. Instead, she'd made friends with people who bloomed in the spotlight.

"So, have you both come down to help figure out what happened to Roger?" Lisa asked, intrigued. She'd never even met someone who'd been involved in a serious crime, and here she was having a chat with three women who had actually had a hand in solving murders. And all while just being ordinary citizens.

"Absolutely," Jane nodded.

"Well, we're here for Abby first and foremost," Eveline answered. "But we'll see what happens."

"They are absolutely not here for that." Abby warned. "And you both better not think of dragging Lisa into this mess."

Lisa finished her cup of tea. "You know, after hearing all this, and after the day we had yesterday, I could do with a proper drink."

Abby watched Jane's face brighten up at the prospect of a girly night.

"I've got wine in the fridge," Abby offered.

"Or, we could go to the pub?" Lisa suggested.

"Oh that sounds like much more fun," Jane said, standing up.

"Jane, you only just got here." Abby protested.

With everything Lisa had just learned, she felt a strong intuitive push to get out, and see what other people were saying. "I'll come clean," she said. "Roger was my friend. Yes, he was a bit of a ladies' man, and he was a daft sod, but he was good to me. He always had time for me, and I feel like I owe it to him to go and give him a send-off. I'm sure that's what they'll be doing in his local pub tonight."

"Oh Abby," Jane said, always the one to offer support first. "She needs some company to mourn the loss of her friend.

Abby wasn't keen, but what could she do? Something terrible had happened, and it may be true that Lisa was much more affected by the tragedy than Abby was, but that didn't mean that Abby didn't need to get over the discovery in her own way. And Abby's way was to allow herself to wallow in the sadness for a bit, allow herself to feel all of her feelings, and then gently re-introduce herself to the world. The thought of going out to the pub was counter-intuitive for her.

"It may well do you some good," Eveline said, keen to see the pub, and maybe learn some more about the man himself.

With three against one, Abby knew there was no point arguing further. "Fine," she relented. "But when I say it's time to go, it's time to go, okay?"

Chapter Thirteen

Abby hadn't been to The Bull pub before, but it looked like a typical English pub from the outside: brick built and square looking. Inside, the décor was similar to other pubs, reds and woods featured strongly.

The pub was centred around the bar, beams cutting it up into sections where tables and chairs were dotted about. Most of the tables were full and the pub was buzzing with talk of Roger's death. It seemed as if the whole town had now heard the news, and each person had come to their own conclusion on who could have killed Roger.

As Lisa walked in with Abby, Jane and Eveline, she was almost mobbed as people recognized her as being not only Roger's friend, but also one of the first people to have found him. Everyone wanted to hear first-hand evidence of what had happened, how Roger was found and what the police had said.

Jane and Eveline pushed their way through to the bar to order drinks, leaving Abby and Lisa to the throbbing mob. Drinks in hand, they found a table set back from the bar. Eveline sat and poured the wine into tall, white wine glasses while Jane went to try to rescue Abby and Lisa.

"Wow, it's crazy in here," Lisa said, as they finally made their way to the table. She sat down on one of the cushioned chairs, taking one of the glasses of wine and taking a long sip. "I knew it was going to be busy, but I had no idea it would be this mobbed."

"Everyone wants to know what happened," Eveline said, looking around at all the animated faces, some sad, some serious, some even looking excitable.

"We should use this opportunity to see what people are thinking," Jane suggested.

"What do you mean?" Lisa asked, leaning in.

There were lots of groups milling about and Abby was feeling a bit hemmed in, particularly as there was one group standing right by her chair, nudging up against the back of it.

"You want to find out who did this to your friend, right?" Eveline asked, seemingly not bothered by the noise and closeness of others. She did lower her voice though, not wanting others to hear her plan.

"Yes, I do," Lisa answered.

"Right now, the police are going to be compiling all the witness statements and asking lots of questions to the people who Roger knew or spent his last few days around. They need an idea of what happened, or what could have happened, in the run up to his demise. And the more information they get, the more they can piece together Roger's movements and try to pinpoint potential suspects. But the number one thing they need to do their job is information, agree?"

Lisa nodded. Abby sat back in her chair. She had a feeling she knew exactly where this was going, and she wasn't entirely sure she wanted to be a part of another murder investigation.

"We have a bit of an advantage on the police right now," Eveline continued. She'd picked up on Abby's hesitancy, but she'd also noticed Lisa's face when Eveline asked her if she wanted to find out what had happened to Roger. "Everyone's had a couple of drinks, people feel relaxed and comfortable, and everyone seems to be in a very chatty mood."

"I guess, but so what?" Lisa asked, wanting to know what she had to do.

"So, we go and talk. Find out what people are saying, see if anything sticks out or hangs together. We need a timeline, that's how you find out what happened to your friend." Eveline explained. Pausing, she let her suggestion sink in. She could tell from Lisa's thoughtful expression that she was digesting what she'd just been told.

Feeling like she'd paused for long enough, Eveline carried on. "You have to track back from last night, and somehow retrace his steps. Who did he fall out with, what was he up to? We need to cut through all the unimportant bits to find the key that will open up the story of what actually happened to your friend."

Lisa looked puzzled. "What, so we go and ask everyone where they were and get their alibis?"

"No," Eveline stopped Lisa. "People will shut down if they think they're in trouble. We don't want to come off as accusing people of anything. We just want to hear what people are saying."

"I don't get it," Lisa said, struggling to understand what she was supposed to be doing.

As much as she didn't want to get involved, Abby found herself leaning back in again. "What Eveline means," she found herself saying, "is that people are talking about Roger. Someone in this pub who's gossiping right now, might actually know who killed him. They just don't know it yet."

"But how are we supposed to know?" Lisa asked.

"We're not. You pay attention, take mental notes, and then after, you try to put them all back together again." Abby explained, knowing Eveline's process by now.

"You don't know what you know until you know it." Eveline added, cryptically.

"I'm confused," Lisa said.

Jane patted Lisa on the arm. "Ignore these two. They have a knack for making things more complicated than they have to be. All they want you to do is go and mingle, talk about Roger, how you can't believe what has happened and who could have done such a thing. Only if you can though, dear. It might be too much to ask right now." Jane was suddenly aware that Lisa might not be up to any type of snooping, and what they were suggesting was somewhat distasteful.

Lisa shifted her weight in the chair, feeling conflicted. "I am devastated by what happened, and I do miss him like crazy. And while one part of me wants to just go home and grieve for him, another part of me wants to fight for him, for the truth. I need to know what happened, and if talking to people and reminiscing about a man I loved will get me one step closer to being able to do that, then I'll do it. Roger wasn't a saint, not by any means, but he didn't deserve the end he met with."

"No-one deserves that, dear." Eveline said. "A human being died before their time, and that's hardly ever an okay thing to happen."

"Hardly ever?" Abby picked up on Eveline's words, raising an eyebrow.

Lucy ran through in her head how she could start a

conversation, practicing her opening line as she took another long sip of wine before asking, "Shall I go and do this then?"

"Well, you're not doing it alone," Jane said, reassuringly.

They decided that they should split up. Lisa and Jane would do the rounds. Eveline decided to use strengths and given Jane was the chattiest amongst them she sent Jane with Lisa, as both seemed far better suited to random conversations. Much to Abby's relief, she was nominated to sit and sip quietly and eavesdrop on any and all conversations happening around them.

With roles assigned, the two groups split. Lisa found the conversation part of the assignment easy, but retaining the information wasn't so straightforward. In the end, she pulled out her phone and opened up the notes app, making quick notes of anything she learned about Roger, and who had commented.

Lisa wasn't stupid, she knew the man liked the ladies and just from the last few nights, she knew he was having affairs with women in town. Heck, at one point, Roger had even got himself banned from the pub last year when a Christmas quiz night had ended in him being knocked out by the pub landlord. Roger had been caught kissing the landlord's wife.

He had gotten away with it that time, but Lisa couldn't help but wonder whether another jealous husband could have taken things a step too far. And it seemed like she wasn't alone in thinking that.

Several people Lisa spoke to, even though she hadn't seen them at any of the advent events, were aware of the two fights Roger had been in. Rumours were rife that maybe one of the husbands or boyfriends had lost their senses and taken steps that had ended in Roger's death.

By the time Jane and Lisa had been to every table, the bell was ringing for last orders. Jane made her way back to the table, as the bar started clearing out, people choosing to leave early.

"I don't think I've talked so much in ages," Jane said, collapsing into her chair. "And my feet are killing me from all the standing up."

Abby topped up Jane's glass with wine, which Jane gratefully took, her throat dry from all the chatting.

"Did you find out anything useful?" Eveline asked, amused at Jane's chatting comment.

"Hmmm, well your man was a serial cheater it seems. Which is awful, as you know I don't like talking ill of the dead." Jane said.

"We were hearing the same thing," Abby agreed. "Everyone thinks it was a jealous husband."

"If only they could all agree on which jealous husband," Eveline added.

Having had their fill of both wine and gossip, they decided to retire for the night. They took a taxi back to Abby's, dropping Lisa off en route. Lisa agreed to head back over to Abby's for breakfast and a regroup the next morning.

By the time Abby walked through her front door she was ready for bed, and she wasn't the only one.

"Shall we head up, run through everything in the morning?" Eveline suggested. "I'm cream crackered!"

Chapter Fourteen

Door 11: The Hotel

Abby came down to freshly-brewed coffee in the morning, with the smell of bacon wafting into the hallway. Eveline passed Abby a fresh cup of coffee as Jane placed a plate of bacon rolls on the kitchen island.

Looking around her kitchen, it looked like Eveline and Jane had been up for some time. They had notebooks set out on the island, with random pieces of paper strewn about.

"Hey Mum," Abby heard Luke's voice before she saw him. He was lounging on the 2-seater in the nook area, book in hand.

"I didn't see you there," Abby said. "How come you're up so early?" She wasn't used to seeing her teenage boys before midday if they didn't have school the next day.

"I smelt bacon," Luke admitted, no other reason needed for a growing boy.

Right on cue, the front doorbell rang and Jane went out into the hallway to let Lisa in.

"Now I feel bad for only just having got up," Abby said, as Lisa walked in.

"I couldn't sleep," Lisa said, pulling her coat off and taking the proffered coffee from Eveline. She moved over to the other side of the kitchen island, taking the fourth stool.

"Have you brought your notes from last night?" Eveline asked.

Lisa nodded, holding up her phone.

They spent the next 2 hours combining all the notes they'd made from their conversations last night in the pub. First, they put them into 3 piles: rumours they'd overheard about other affairs and upset husbands; conversations they heard related to the 2 fights Abby and Lisa had witnessed; and any conversation snippets that could give them an idea of timeline.

Next, they went through all the snippets about other affairs, of which there were a fair few. There were lots of names bandied around, but they couldn't yet tell whether there was any truth in the rumours. They moved on to the conversations touching on the fights.

More coffee was needed at that point and Luke, who had been relaxing on the sofa pretending to read, was drafted in as coffee maker.

The timeline they managed to come up with was scant. They knew Roger had been at Day 2's advent door and day 5's, but his comings and goings around those 2 events were still somewhat of a mystery. Lisa had left him at the bottom of her street after he'd walked her most of the way home after she'd broken up his first fight, but she hadn't seen him since.

After scouring through every tidbit of information,

from rumours of his affairs with half the golf club, to conjecture about him having fathered several children over the years, they'd come to a dead end. The picture of Roger they'd wanted to end this session with wasn't quite as full as they'd have liked.

Lisa couldn't help but feel dejected. "I don't know what I expected to discover," she admitted. "I know murders aren't solved in a day, but I wanted to feel like there was something there that we hadn't known before, you know?"

Abby shrugged sympathetically. She could tell Lisa wanted answers, but she also knew that they were often the hardest things to come by. "How about we break for lunch?" she suggested.

"Marvellous idea," Jane said, perking up at the mention of food.

Eveline sat back, looking at the information they'd written on all the post its. She grabbed the pile and took it over to the other side of the kitchen, where Luke was still sitting on the couch.

"Luke, come here and help me," Eveline said, struggling to move a plant pot out of the way so she could have a clear expanse of wall.

Eveline started putting up the post its. "You see," she said, turning around, her eyes searching Lisa out. "We know things already. We know much more than we did yesterday."

Lisa walked over to where Eveline was standing, her hand reaching out and brushing over the little blue post it notes that she'd written out. They were now grouped with the other coloured post-it notes on Abby's kitchen wall, making up a kind of picture view of all their knowledge.

"Here," Eveline said, pointing to one. "Everyone had 'potential affairs' stories about Roger, but I didn't hear one person call him out for malicious behaviour or anything other than the fact that he was a ladies' man."

"I guess," Lisa said, not seeing the significance.

"Sometimes, what isn't said tells us more than what is," Eveline explained.

"Ok?" Lisa responded, still unsure what Eveline was trying to tell her.

"There's nothing else untoward, which means we're not picking up on any other motive right now, other than the affairs one."

"Right," Lisa said, a lightbulb switching on. "So, it means that we focus on the affair angle, right?"

"Precisely. Everyone's talking about all these rumours, and we almost want to run through them all and dismiss them."

"Dismiss them? But that's all we've got?" Lisa was feeling confused again.

"They're just rumours right now, conjecture. Right now, we know about 2 affairs that were fact, right?" Eveline persisted.

"We do."

"So, those are our next stops. If we're hearing nothing else, then maybe that's because there is nothing else."

"You mean we're looking for something other than rumoured affairs? But all there is is rumoured affairs, so stop looking for other things and focus on closing them out?"

"Precisely. You never know though, those other things might come up once we start putting some context around the affairs."

"But we have a place to start?" Lisa asked.

"Right."

Abby could sense a charge rush through the atmosphere, almost like a spark of electricity changed the whole feel of the room from one of despondency to one of anticipation. "Why don't I make us some quick sandwiches, and then maybe we could go and speak to the women involved in those 2 fights?"

"I know Alan's wife," Lisa said, her voice becoming more energetic as she felt the shift towards something positive. "She's a hairdresser in town. Shall we maybe start with her?"

Chapter Fifteen

They caught Alan's wife, Jenny, on her lunch break at the salon. She was sitting at the desk near the front entrance, drinking a coffee. The salon was almost empty. Two older women were seated at the far end, sitting reading magazines as they waited for their colours to take.

The pure whiteness of the salon interior made Abby's head fuzzy. Even the staff were wearing white, which Abby found unusual as every other hairdresser she'd been to opted for more of a black theme.

Maybe Jenny was going for an opposite look, Abby noted, as they were led through into the back. "I don't want any talk around the old biddies back there. Worst gossips in the whole town. Five minutes after any conversation in here and the whole ruddy retirement village up the road knows about it. I sure as heck don't want any more of my personal business getting out."

Once they were safely tucked away in the back office, all crowded round the desk that took up most of the floor space, Jenny was more than happy to talk. She seemed almost thrilled at the prospect of someone fighting over her.

Abby perched on top of a tower of boxes that sat in the corner. Along the whole back of the wall boxes were stacked, filled with various hair products if the labels on the front were accurate. There was barely room to swing a cat between the oversized desk and all the boxed products.

"It had sort of fizzled out between me and Andy, you know," Jenny started, as she took the comfy-looking white leather chair behind the desk. Behind her were huge black and white portraits, one of just Jenny, and the other of 2 fluffy cats.

"So, do you think Alan could have lost his rag and killed Roger?" Lisa asked, getting right to the point.

"My Alan's not much of a fighting man," Jenny said, shaking her head.

Abby thought back to that first fight she'd witnessed Roger in. She had to agree with Jenny. Neither Alan nor Roger looked like they would have lasted a minute in a boxing ring.

"And can Alan account for his whereabouts the night Roger was killed?" Eveline asked, wanting something more than the wife's opinion of the husband to rule Alan out as a suspect.

"Thing is," Jenny explained, licking her lips. "Al's never done anything like that for me before, you know. I've never seen him fight anyone before. He's so laid back he can hardly get off the couch usually, you know."

Abby was beginning to wonder whether Jenny was able to end a sentence without the words 'you know' added onto the end.

"He told me what happened, came home that night all dishevelled, you know." Jenny continued.

Abby felt a sudden urge to comment on all the 'you know's. She held her tongue.

"Best make-up sex I've ever had, you know." Jenny said.

"No, I don't know at all, thankfully." Eveline quipped.

"Huh?" Jenny looked confused for a minute. It didn't take long for her to resume her story though. "Every night since, you know, we've been indoors by 6pm and we've been rocking that house until we have no more rocking left in us."

"Charming," Eveline muttered.

"Well done you, dear," Jane piped up, enjoying watching Eveline squirm.

"So, he has an alibi then?" Eveline confirmed.

"Oh, he has an alibi alright," Jenny said, winking.

Abby was just impressed Jenny had been able to withhold a 'you know'.

By the time they got out of the hairdressers, Eveline and Abby both had headaches coming on.

"Every sentence," Eveline groaned. "It took every ounce of self-restraint to not teach that woman some elocution tips.

"What are you two moaning about?" Lisa asked, completely unphased by Jenny's habit.

"Don't tell me you didn't notice how the woman ended every sentence?" Abby asked, amazed.

"It's just a habit," Lisa explained kindly. "We all have them, and we'll all irritate people with them. You've just got to learn to let them wash over you if you're going to have any peace."

Abby and Eveline exchanged a glance, feeling like they'd been told off. Abby noticed how Lisa never seemed to have a bad word to say about anyone. As far as she was concerned this non-reaction was just unnatural. "I've never asked, but what is it you do for a living?"

"Why do you ask?" Lisa said, wondering where the

question came from.

"I don't know really. It just struck me that you always seem to stick up for people. I wondered whether it might have something to do with whatever you do for a living."

Lisa chuckled. "It might do," she admitted. "I'm a life coach."

"Oooh, do you want to life coach me?" Jane asked, intrigued. She might be getting on in years, but Jane was sure she still had a few tricks she could learn.

They'd learned a little more about Roger from quizzing Jenny. She'd met him through the accountancy firm she used. He'd been her accountant for four years now, and her lover for 18 months apparently. Jane had commented that their affair had lasted longer than most of her long-term relationships, much to the amusement of Jenny.

Chapter Sixteen

Abby was surprised to find it was almost 4pm when she looked at her watch. "Shoot!" she said. "I've volunteered for tonight's door. I'm gonna have to go and get ready."

"They're still having it?" Eveline asked, surprised the event hadn't been cancelled.

"They had a meeting last night to decide whether to cancel the rest of the doors, but Roger wouldn't have wanted that apparently. And his daughter, Clarissa, gave her blessing for the event to continue."

"Wow," Eveline said, equally impressed and surprised.

"I think because so many small companies have put in such an effort," Abby said. "And cancelling won't bring Roger back, and it won't speed up an arrest either."

"The show must go in," Jane added.

"Exactly," Lisa agreed. "The show must go on. Besides, these shows raise the profile of all these clubs which is a good thing for the community, and we're supporting lots of local charities too."

"Really?" Jane asked, unaware of the charity angle.

"Yes, they invite a different charity to each different

event. They have one or two volunteers attend, with collection buckets. Just one more reason why I wanted to get involved this year." Lisa said.

"Do you know what's on tonight then?" Eveline asked.

Abby looked blankly at Lisa. "You know, I have no idea," she admitted.

"Me neither." Lisa said. "I'm supposed to be volunteering too tonight, but I don't really have very much Christmas cheer left. Do you think they'll struggle with one man down?"

"Me and Eveline could stand in for you, dear," Jane offered.

"That would be so kind if you could. Maybe I can try to find out where Roxanne will be in the morning, and we can go meet her and ask some more questions?" Lisa offered.

"Sounds like a plan." Eveline said.

"Get some rest, dear, and don't worry about tonight." Jane said, embracing Lisa in a comforting bear hug. "You've done so well today, Roger would be proud of you."

Lisa felt the threat of tears as Jane's soothing words hit her heart hard. "Thank you for helping me do this," she said. "Even if it comes to nothing, it just feels good to be trying to help, you know?"

Abby offered a supportive smile and a hug, pushing a little tube into Lisa's hands. Lisa turned the tube over in her hand, focusing on the label, and offering up a smile in return. It was a mistletoe bath salts mix.

As soon as Hilary saw Abby walking into the

community hub, she ran over. "How's Lisa?" she asked, looking flustered.

Without waiting for a response, Hilary's guilt about going ahead with the event spilled out. "I'm just not sure we've made the right decision. It just feels wrong to be doing this, to be having fun and bringing joy. It just feels like it should be a time of sadness and sorrow, and I just, I'm not sure this is a good idea."

"Roger's family have given the go ahead, no?" Abby asked.

Hilary nodded.

"So, you have their blessing. And if they say it's okay, then it's okay. And if they'd have said it wasn't, then the event would have been cancelled, right? You've done the right thing Hilary, don't worry."

Throughout the event that night, Abby noticed how fidgety and distracted Hilary was, but the event went ahead without cause for concern. And it almost seemed like the event for that night was serendipitous.

Abby, as usual, waited outside the local hotel with her light stick, directing people indoors to a function room in the back of the hotel. The local Nepalese community were hosting the door's event. Sharing a different side of the Folkesdowne community, Abby hadn't realized how many Nepalese families lived in this little part of Kent, all based around the British Army Gurkha division.

Traditional food was laid out on some tables to the side of the stage, but all eyes were focused on the stage. Women dressed in beautiful red, flowing outfits with ornate gold jewellery adorning their necks, ears and wrists, came out and stood statuesque, on the stage. The Maruni, a traditional dance popular in Nepal, was performed. The audience was encouraged to clap and dance along to the music, which some of the younger kids did without prompting. Abby watched, mesmerised, as the women performed intricate movements, weaving around each other with a grace she was pretty sure she could never replicate.

As the dance ended to a huge round of applause, a couple of the dancers came down from the stage and gave an introduction to some basic moves of the Maruni, before inviting everyone to try them out.

Abby was not surprised to see Jane and Eveline down in the front, giving it their all. She was amazed at how agile they both still were, both women being in their '70s, although both were far fitter than Abby considered herself to be.

Standing on the edge of the dance floor, trying to hide behind the mask of stewardship, giving off the air of enjoyment but with a job to do. Abby thought she'd got away with trying out any of the dance moves, but that was until Hilary appeared at her side.

"Come on, Abby," Hilary said, her whole body now a picture of relaxed merriment. "Show us your moves, woman."

Abby gave it her best shot, feeling completely self-conscious throughout the whole sorry attempt, moving back into a position of official watcher as soon as she could. Whilst the act of dancing was not for her, Abby loved watching people trying out the moves, smiling and having fun and letting their bodies move. It felt like wholesome fun, just what the doctor had ordered after the last event.

Jane and Eveline finally made their way back to Abby with plates full of delicious-looking Nepalese food. Abby recognized the samosas and gratefully took one from Jane, who had also brought over a plate of delicacies that Abby didn't know the name of.

Thankfully, that's where Jane came in. Abby had no idea how she'd learned the names of each dish, but Jane was able to point out the Wo pancakes, the little envelopes of white flour stuffed with minced lamb that were called Momos, and some Dal Bhat, which was the Nepalese staple of rice served with lentil soup and vegetable curry.

"I've had such a wonderful evening," Jane said, as they made their way upstairs after another eventful night.

"It was really good, wasn't it?" Abby agreed.

"Every town should do this," Eveline added. "It's just so good for the soul, meeting new people and having chats with people you'd never normally engage with. I loved it all."

Eveline must have enjoyed it, Abby thought, noting that not one mention was made of Roger and the plans for the next day's investigative activities.

Chapter Seventeen

Door 12 – The Shopping Centre

That had all changed by the morning, and Eveline and Jane were keen to get back to Folkesdowne and interview the woman involved in the second fight.

Swigging down a cup of tea and munching through some jam on toast, they left Abby's before nine am, making their way to a café they'd arranged to meet Lisa at. It also happened to be the café where Roxanne Davies, Lance's fiancé, worked.

Roxanne recognized Abby as soon as they walked in, an embarrassed look taking the place of her ready smile. As Jane sat at an empty table, Roxanne rushed over, keen to avoid any further embarrassment.

Lisa welcomed Roxanne over with a warm smile. "How are you, Roxie?" she asked.

Abby took the lead, wanting to put Roxie at ease. "I hope everything was resolved with your boyfriend?"

Abby asked.

Roxie answered hesitantly, "Yes, thanks."

"We just wondered whether you'd be willing to answer a few questions we have?"

"Why?" Roxie challenged. Her whole body language suddenly became closed off and defensive, her arms crossing tightly across her chest, her back straightening, her chest puffed out.

"I'm trying to find out what happened to Roger, Rox." Lisa explained. "These women are trying to help me."

"Won't the police do that?" Roxie asked.

"Yes, but who knows how long that will take," Lisa said. "And I don't know what they'll tell me when they solve the case. More than anything I just want to understand it all, make sense of it in my own way."

Roxie seemed to relax a little. "I can give you ten minutes."

"That's all we need," Abby said. "Thank you."

Roxie went back to the serving station to let the other server know she was taking a break. She returned to the table with a tray laden with cups, a milk jug, sugar bowl and a large teapot.

She sat down on the last remaining chair at the rectangular table. Jane took control of serving the tea before pulling a hot pink notebook from her oversized shoulder bag.

Eveline took over at that point, a list of questions ready to fire off. "Just to rule things out and try to get a better picture of who could have had it out for Roger, could you explain the relationship between the two of you."

Roxanne sat back in her chair, playing nervously with her hands that lay, fidgeting, in her lap. "Lance and I, about 6 months ago, we had a massive fight. Can't even remember how it started now, just one of those blow up fights."

Eveline nodded, silently encouraging Roxie to continue with her story.

"Anyway," Rosie continued. "We split up for a couple of weeks. One night, after I'd had one too many, I decided I needed to get over Lance and so went on an old dating app I used to use. And up popped Roger. We chatted some and once we worked out we were in the same tiny town, well, it seemed crazy not to meet up."

"Makes perfect sense," Jane said, imagining herself in a similar situation.

"Yes, it did to me too," Roxie said. "But one thing led to another and we started a relationship, well more like a casual relationship, if you know what I mean."

"Oh yes, dear," Jane nodded. "Sometimes, they're the best kind."

Lisa sniggered, unable to stop a little snort escape her lips.

Roxie looked perplexed. Abby assumed the woman couldn't make her mind up about Jane, wondering whether she was being authentic or not. If only Roxie knew this was Jane in her calm state, Abby thought. "It was all just so easy, no drama. Roger was lovely, very affectionate. He made me feel good about myself, and I needed that."

Lisa knew exactly what Roxie meant. He made Lisa feel the same way, which made her wonder why their relationship had always remained platonic.

"As you can guess, Lance and I got back together again, but he's so uptight. Roger's just such a different bloke, and I found it hard to give that up."

"So Lance found out?"

"Yes. The thing is, I want to settle down, maybe have

a baby or two. And Roger isn't the kind of guy who settles. Lance, on the other hand, most definitely is. So while my heart was making me do one thing, my head was making me do another."

"And how did Lance take it all?" Eveline asked.

"Not amazingly well, as you can imagine," Roxie admitted. "But if you're wondering whether Lance killed Roger, there's no way."

"And how can you be sure of that?" Eveline pushed.

"I, I can't, I guess. Not rationally anyway. I mean, technically, sure, I guess he could have, but that's just not Lance. No way."

"So, can I just ask whether you both left immediately after the altercation with Roger at the bandstand?"

"We did. And we spent the whole night thrashing it out. Lance wanted space, to go home by himself. But I knew if he did, he'd leave me. So I made him come back to my place and I laid my heart out on the table."

"And what about the night of the railway event?" Abby asked.

"He was with me," Roxanne said.

"So, you're his alibi?" Eveline confirmed.

"Yes, I guess I am."

"So, when you said that technically he could have killed Roger?" Abby wasn't sure what it was, couldn't put her finger on anything particular, but she felt a hesitancy in Roxanne's voice when she accepted she was Lance's alibi. Was she really or was she covering for him?

"Yeah, no, he logically couldn't." Roxanne interrupted. "Because he couldn't have been in two places at the same time. Sorry."

"Thank you, Roxie. I know you didn't have to sit down with us and relive that night. I'm really grateful to you for sharing," Lisa said.

"Not at all, Lisa. And I really am sorry for your loss. As I said, Roger was a lovely guy."

"He really was," Lisa said quietly, emotion choking her throat.

Abby reached over, placing a hand on Lisa's forearm. "You okay?"

Back at Abby's after their hunt for the men involved in the two fights – Alan and Lance – was unsuccessful, they found out where Alan worked and arranged to meet up with Lisa again and drop by Alan's work to ask him a few questions.

With the evening stretching out ahead of them, Jane and Eveline accompanied Abby to that night's advent event. Door number 12 was held in the shopping centre and featured several local dance groups who had come together to create a song and dance Christmas melody. There was even a Christmas dragon dance, though Abby had to admit to knowing nothing about where that idea came from.

Abby's favourite dance was by the local ballet and tap school, who did an amazingly intricate performance of Frosty the Snowman partaking in a 'singing in the rain' type parody, retitled with new lyrics as Sledging in the Snow. Jane still had the song stuck in her head three hours later when they were getting ready to go up to bed.

Chapter Eighteen

Door 13: The Community Centre

It came as a surprise to Abby the next morning when she heard Jane's dulcet tones still singing the Frosty/Sledging in the Snow mash up.

"Why are you still singing that?" Abby asked, laughing as she walked into the kitchen to be confronted by Jane watching herself in the mirror with a croissant in her hand in place of a microphone.

"It's a catchy tune," Jane said, spinning around and greeting Abby with a grin.

"It really isn't," Eveline moaned, sitting at the kitchen island with a book, trying in vain to read a page with the singing interruptions from Jane.

"Well, it must be catchy, because I can't stop singing it."

"Please try," Abby said, not sure she could put up with the singing for any length of time. Not only was she finding the tune now playing on repeat in her own head, but she was seriously wondering whether to break it to Jane that she was no Mariah Carey.

Unfortunately, Jane was still humming the tune to herself as they made their way into the market. Thankfully, Christmas songs were playing over a speaker system and Jane soon swapped to humming a different tune.

They found Alan picking up an older lady's fruit and vegetables and rearranging her trolley so her bread was on top and wouldn't get squashed.

"Alan?" Lisa grabbed his attention and he smiled widely, looking like he didn't have a care in the world. "Got a sec?"

Alan wandered over. "How can I help you ladies?"

"We're actually here about my friend, Roger," Lisa said.

The colour quickly drained out of Alan's face. "I'm so sorry for your loss. That was just awful. I can't believe it was just a few days ago, when we saw each other."

"About that," Lisa said, an encouraging nudge from Eveline prompting her to take the lead. "I don't know whether you remember, it was me and Abby who broke up the fight you and Roger were having."

Alan laughed. "I don't think anyone could call that a fight, do you?"

"So you didn't kill him then?" Jane asked, making sure to set her tone as jovial and jokey.

"Roger?" Alan asked. "Heck no, I owe that man a debt."

"How so?" Lisa asked.

"Turns out Jenny found out I confronted Roger, she

loved it. I mean, before, we were just going through the motions, not really connecting. I don't even think we fancied each other anymore. It was just tired. But that completely changed when someone told her I'd confronted Roger."

"Really?" Lisa wondered how news of the fight had got out so quickly.

"If I'd known all I needed to do was act more like a caveman, heck, I would have done that years ago. And there was me trying to be all sensitive and caring."

Abby felt like feminism had taken about ten steps back just by listening to Alan's story, feeling slightly horrified at Jenny's reaction. "I take it you have an alibi for the night Roger was killed then?"

"Oh yes, a pretty special one too," Alan said, winking smugly.

Abby felt offended for women everywhere, having decided that Alan was a bit of a letch.

"Wow, that man was full on, wasn't he?" Jane said as they left the market.

"Wasn't he just!" Eveline agreed.

They decided to stop en route to intercept Lance leaving his workplace for the day and headed to a café for a cuppa. There was plenty of time to still get to the offices Lance worked in, but when they arrived at Lance's office, they discovered he hadn't been there all day.

The secretary at the front desk leaned in towards the women as she told them that Lance had called in, as he'd had to go in and give a statement to the police. "He said it wouldn't take too long and to expect him to be an hour or so late, but he never turned up." The secretary looked positively gleeful at having some part to play in a murder investigation.

"Is he due in tomorrow?" Lisa asked, wondering if

they'd be able to catch him the next day.

"Should be unless he's still being held. Gosh, you don't think he did it, do you?"

"Time will tell I guess." Abby said, wondering herself.

Deciding it would be best to catch up with Lance on a different day, they went back to their notes, updating what they'd found out in the various interviews they had. All they discovered was that they were quickly coming to a dead end. Other than Lance, they'd interviewed the other couples involved in the disagreements. Jenny and Alan were each other's alibis, and while technically Alan could have planned the whole thing and got Jenny to cover for him, having met them both, it just didn't seem plausible. True, they hadn't spoken to Lance yet, but having heard Roxie's side of the story, that too looked like nothing would come of it.

Eveline suggested they go back to their notes from the pub, thinking maybe something would come up now that they knew a bit more. At which point, Jane pointed out the obvious: it was time to learn more about Roger. And Lisa was their first point of call.

Having left Lisa back in Folkesdowne, Abby called and asked if she was going to that evening's event. Lisa ummed and aahed, not feeling ready for it, but once Abby explained that they needed to know more about Roger, Lisa agreed to attend and give them as much detail as she could.

Day 13's door was in the local bingo hall, that was more of a community hall used for lots of different functions. When the hall wasn't putting on its twice-weekly bingo events, there was ballroom dancing, art and yoga classes and even street dance classes.

Jane's eyes widened when they walked into the hall to find tables set out, a collection of bingo pens and cards in the middle of each table.

"My mum used to play bingo religiously," Jane said, getting nostalgic.

Each person was to receive three cards free, and then if they wanted more they had to make a donation. Jane ended up with six cards in total, and Abby had never seen her so quiet, concentrating on the bingo caller sitting up at the front of the hall, her bingo machine set to start. In keeping with the theme, the room had been decorated with gold and green tinsel, with baubles hanging down from tacks on the ceiling. The bingo caller had even dressed up as Mrs Claus, and she had two elves helping her.

Abby quickly realized that this was absolutely the wrong event to get Lisa talking, but she noted that as Lisa walked in to join the people already taking their seats, she looked relieved at the set up. Jane waved Lisa over and she took the free chair opposite Eveline and Jane, grabbing her bingo cards and pen. Abby was standing to the side, in her hi-viz jacket, on hand to help anyone who needed it.

When the second person called a line, Abby looked over to see Eveline nibbling at her fingers and looking anxiously at Mrs Claus.

"Two little duckies, twenty-two," Mrs Claus called out.

"House!" Eveline shouted excitedly, standing up and waving her bingo card in the air. "I've won!" she shouted as groans of disappointment could be heard from all those who were waiting for one or two numbers for their own house.

Chapter Nineteen

Door 14: The Installation

They finally found Lance the next day at his local, propping up the bar and in a foul mood after being questioned for hours the day before over his involvement in Roger's death. Given that he was already drunk and it wasn't even midday, Abby approached carefully. He was talking to everyone and anyone about his encounter with the law yesterday, and Abby wasn't sure they'd get any logical or reliable answers out of him. Jane had other ideas, reasoning that a chatty, drunk man would say things that a sober man would not, and they'd be able to separate the hyperbole from the truth without a problem.

While Abby and Eveline were ready to leave as soon as they saw the state Lance was in, Jane insisted on buying the poor man a drink and asking him to sit and have a chat. Lance was happy to do anything for another pint, but didn't realise Jane had swapped out his ale order for a low alcohol option.

Lisa was on the fence. She felt bad quizzing a man who obviously didn't have his wits about him, but her need to find out what had happened to Roger was stronger than any feeling of unfairness.

Jane asked her first question. "Do you remember what happened the night you had the fight with Roger?" and Lance crumbled. His bottom lip quivered as he sniffled, emotion and alcohol a ready mix for an emotional explosion.

"She broke my heart, did my Rox," Lance said, tears he'd been holding onto starting to spill onto his t-shirt.

Jane looked over at Abby and Eveline aghast, and Lisa sunk down low in her chair, wishing she was anywhere but where she was.

Feeling massively sorry for Lance, Abby couldn't help but feel a little smug when looking at Jane, who was wondering how to handle the situation she'd gotten herself into. Did she not know that trying to have an intelligent conversation with a heartbroken drunk man was the worse thing you could do?

"I asked her to marry me, that woman was the love of my life" Lance was saying.

Jane found herself left with no other option than to cast off any ideas of getting anywhere on the interview front, and instead provide a warm and friendly shoulder to cry on. "Some women just don't deserve a good man, my dear."

As was usual with the average British man, taught from an early age to hide any vulnerable feelings away and turn to alcohol instead, finding someone who was giving him the space he needed to feel his feelings, it was an almost cathartic experience for Lance.

Lisa ended up leaving Jane and Lance to it and moving

across to Abby and Eveline's table. Thankfully, the lunch rush never came, and so the two tables were left in peace for the next two hours. Abby ordered food, sending a sharing platter over to Jane's table, which both Jane and Lance gratefully munched through.

"She's amazing," Lisa said, watching as Jane emphasized with Lance's situation, working the conversation in such a way as to allow Lance himself to realise what should be his next steps with his relationship.

Having grudgingly agreed to stay at the pub, smugly enjoying Jane's discomfort when her conversation with Lance had blown up, Abby now marvelled at how easy Jane seemed to find it to connect with people. More than that though, Jane seemed able to show people how to connect to themselves, which Lisa had also picked up on.

"After all this is over, I am going to sit down with that woman and pick her brains about everything." Lisa said.

Lance went from an emotional wreck to realizing he had the power over how he felt, and how he allowed others to make him feel, and an understanding that hurt and betrayal are perfectly natural healthy emotions to have.

Lance left the pub a little bit soberer and a whole lot happier, and Jane was rewarded for her efforts with pats on the back and a huge plate of chips with tomato ketchup and mayonnaise.

"I have to say," Lisa said as Jane stuffed a few chips into her mouth. "I'm in awe of how you just handled that situation, Jane. You really turned that conversation around."

"I should have listened to you guys and left him be," Jane admitted. "I guess I did come away with a real sense of the guy. And that, coupled with the fact that he told me what happened after the fight, and his story corroborates Roxie's, I think we can leave poor Lance off our suspect list."

"What did he say about how Roxanne dealt with the aftermath, then?" Abby asked, curious as to the status of their relationship.

"The poor guy is madly in love. But they're not even married yet, and she's already cheating on him." Jane said, realizing she had a real soft spot for Lance. She wondered whether she could convince him to end his relationship with Roxie and introduce him to some nicer women.

Eveline interrupted her thoughts. "I can see what you're thinking, and have you not learned anything about putting your nose where it doesn't belong?"

"I don't know what you think you know, Eveline, but whatever it is, you're wrong." Jane shot back.

"So you weren't wondering about whether you could split up Roxanne and Lance for good then?"

"I wasn't thinking any such thing. That's ridiculous." Jane said, huffing in irritation as she sat back in her chair, folding her arms across her chest.

Lisa looked from one to another, taking in Jane's stony silence and Eveline's amused condescension. She glanced over at Abby, who happily explained that they were constantly bickering. "I remember being shocked when I witnessed my first row, but now I just see it as they love each other." Abby saw Eveline's over-exaggerated eye roll and chuckled.

Chapter Twenty

Leaving the pub, having crossed the one and only potential remaining suspect off their list, they were back to their plan of quizzing people who knew Roger well, to flesh out the timeline and the man himself. And first on their list was Lisa, who was still to share the story of how and why she and Roger became such good friends.

Lisa had agreed to come back to Abby's and fill in some details about who Roger was, what he did for a living and for fun, and what his lifestyle was like. Eveline was specifically after clues that would give her an idea of where to flesh out his story, leading up to his death. Little details like did he go to the gym, how often did he go to the pub, what were his hobbies, who were his friends, and who did he spend time with were top of Eveline's list. So far, the only picture they had of Roger was based around the two fights and his dalliances with other women. Eveline knew that was only one side of the man, and there were bound to be little details, that when brought together, would give a more rounded picture of Roger's personality and his life.

Walking towards Abby's car, Jane almost bumped into a young girl who was carrying several bags in each hand, all of varying sizes. "Oh, sorry dear," Jane exclaimed as a couple of the bags fell to the floor, their contents spilling out onto the pavement. Jane bent to help, as did the others, but as they all stood back up the girl recognized Lisa.

"Clarissa!" Lisa said, embarrassed that she hadn't recognised Roger's daughter straightaway.

Clarissa and Lisa hugged tightly, before Lisa introduced Clarissa to Jane, Eveline and Abby. "These women are helping me to try and make sense of it all."

"I'm still trying too," Clarissa admitted, tears welling up in her eyes. "They're saying it's because Dad had lots of affairs." Clarissa pulled a tissue out of her coat pocket and blew her nose. "I know he wasn't a saint, but I don't think he'd ever do anything to hurt someone on purpose. And he's single, so he can have relationships. It's not him cheating."

"I know exactly what you mean," Lisa agreed. "It's like they've decided he's a bad guy so he's not worth it, but they just don't know him like we do."

"I'm not pretending he was perfect, but then who is?" Clarissa said, feeling the need to defend her dad's honour.

Lisa told Clarissa how they'd spoken to the two men who'd recently had alterations and how they were trying to work out whether there were any other clues in Roger's life that could explain what happened.

Clarissa gave them some names of people she knew Roger had spent time with regularly, a few of them Lisa had never heard of. Clarissa was also able to tell them a bit about his schedule. Lisa had known that he loved spinning and went to a weekly class, but she hadn't known about his twice-weekly yoga class. She wondered why Roger had never told her about the yoga, she would have gone with him if she'd known. Clarissa also mentioned that he had a standing appointment on a Tuesday evening, though she didn't know what it was for or who it was with.

Promising to raid her dad's calendar and messages on his phone to get details on anything or anyone else she could find, she left them to it, picking up her bags and heading home.

Chapter Twenty-One

They now had a decent list of people and places to check out, and with Lisa adding more details, they set about planning what they would do the next day. It was already getting dark and they decided approaching people in the dark was probably not the best way to proceed. Besides, day fourteen's door was waiting.

Lisa decided to attend that night's event as a volunteer again, alongside Abby. Jane and Eveline refused to miss it, having had such a good time at the other door events. And this one did not disappoint.

The location for the event was seemingly in an abandoned space. The lighting wasn't amazing and Abby had to use the torch facility on her phone to make sure she could see what was in front of her.

As they got close though, they could see why the location had been chosen. The event for that night was a light installation. Different Christmas themed lights had been attached to abandoned buildings. There was a huge square-like light installation in the middle of the lot and small, round light balls dotted around in some kind of pattern. The company who was putting on the show that night were still stress testing all the lights and all the volunteers stood around watching as different lights turned on and off in some form of melodic dance.

It wasn't until all the guests arrived and the music started that Abby understood why they were testing the lights at different time periods. The lights were set to instrumental music, with only a handful of lights lighting up at first as the music started. As the tempo of the music rose up in a searing crescendo, becoming both louder and faster, the lights started to increase. The light balls that were dotted around started changing colour and then letters started appearing on them, spelling out short, positive words, such as love, goodwill and peace to all.

When the music went quiet, so did the lights. And when the music peaked, the lights lit up the night sky, casting warm waves of light across the ground. The square-like structure made of some kind of light beam, came into its own as the show came to an end. A rainbow of colours flashed across all four sides of the square, as a bright yellow star appeared in the middle, glowing brightly.

Once the music died down, people were invited to come into the square and brush their hands up against it, the lights reacting to peoples' touch, moving with them.

"Thought I'd catch you lot here," DI Murray appeared at Abby's side.

"Oh hi, Inspector," Eveline said, chattily.

DI Murphy mumbled something under her breath before launching into her offensive. "Look, I know you're all poking about in this investigation, thinking you're helping, or whatever it is you think you're doing."

"Well if you'd just keep us updated with what's going on, we wouldn't need to find out for ourselves," Lisa argued.

"We have no obligation to keep people updated on our investigation unless you are immediate family. Imagine if that was part of the remit ladies, we'd have to dedicate a resource just to keep people informed. Two guesses whether that would or wouldn't keep us from actually investigating?"

Lisa looked down, realising she'd maybe been out of line. "I get it," she said. "I just can't sleep properly until I know what happened to Roger. Talking about him with people, asking them what they know, it helps."

"And, of course," Eveline added, "if we were to actually stumble across something that was pertinent to the investigation, we would bring it straight to the police."

"And you'd know what was pertinent or not how?" DI Murphy challenged.

"Eveline here used to be in the police force herself," Jane said, defending her friend.

DI Murphy didn't seem too impressed. "As what exactly?"

"I ended my career as a Detective Sergeant, and probably took a heck of a lot longer to get there than it took you."

Abby watched as the information played out on DI Murphy's face. Murphy must have known that being a woman police officer was a hard slog back when Eveline must have been in the force. Things had definitely changed for the better, but even now women had a hard time climbing the ranks.

"Listen," Murphy decided to take a different slant. "I know you want to find out what happened to your friend, but just remember that this is a murder investigation, which means that we still have a killer out there. It would be remiss of me to not say that what you are doing could have some serious ramifications.

"Understood," Eveline said.

DI Murphy made a point to look each woman in the eye before finishing. "I don't need to be adding to my investigation, okay?"

Eveline may have cast off the warning without too much interest, but DI Murphy's warning landed with Abby. She knew the risks, of course she did, but having them spelt out by a police officer seemed to make it so much more serious.

The effect on Lisa hit harder. She looked horrified. Lisa hadn't really considered the fact that looking for the reason for Roger's death also meant looking for the person that caused that death. And what if she found them? What if she found them when she was alone?

As DI Murphy walked away, Lisa found herself asking, "Have you ever met a murderer then?"

All three women answered in the affirmative, which horrified Lisa even more. She really didn't want to meet a killer. The very thought of it sent her heart racing.

"Most killers aren't psychopaths," Eveline said, trying to allay Lisa's concerns. "There's usually a reason for someone killing another person, and they're not likely to just swing for anyone."

"The motive is the thing," Jane added. "I've found there's often a really sad and complicated reason people kill. I mean some, my heart breaks for them when you find out what they've been through." Jane thought back to a recent case.

Abby had to agree. If she'd learned nothing else from her recent investigations with Jane and Eveline, it was that real life was messy, and nothing was ever black and white, nor people good or evil.

Lisa wasn't convinced. And hearing how they'd all had experiences with people who had, for whatever reason, killed another person, Lisa wasn't about to find out how that would feel. "Maybe we've done enough," she said. "Maybe we leave it to the police now, and do what DI Murphy said."

"If that's what you want," Eveline said. "Tell you what, sleep on it. If you feel exactly as you do now in the morning, then we drop the whole thing, okay?"

Chapter Twenty-Two

Door 15: The Refugee Centre

The next morning, over breakfast, as Abby put three mugs of tea on the island and popped some bread into the toaster, she found herself musing over what was said the night before. "So, we may call this quits then?"

"Say again, dear?" Jane said, taking the proffered mug of tea. She touched the stoneware mug with its simple Nordic pattern to her lips, taking a sip.

"I mean, what Eveline said last night," Abby said. "About us leaving the case alone if Lisa doesn't want to pursue it anymore."

"Codswallop," Eveline said. "We're just getting into the details now. We'd be foolish to give up now."

"But what about what Lisa wants?" Abby persisted.

"I am 100% certain that she'll come to her senses, you'll see." Eveline grabbed a slice of toast from the plate Abby placed in the centre of the island.

"But we won't do anything until she gives the go

ahead, right?"

"About that," Eveline hesitated. She knew she was pushing Abby's patience and deliberately going back on her word to Lisa, but her gut was telling her to keep on going. Ignoring her gut always leads to bad things in Eveline's experience. She had to come up with a compromise that would both appease Abby and sit well with her own conscience. And she had the perfect idea.

Meaning they wouldn't lose time, but also ensuring they didn't completely let go of the investigative work, Eveline suggested they go into Folkesdowne and do some last minute shopping. With only ten days left until Christmas, they could all do with adding to their Christmas gift supplies. Eveline's plan was to then unleash Jane on a charm offensive. Jane would be sent into the shops where they'd already worked out there was a contact of some form to Roger. Jane, being as chatty as can be, would ask about news of Roger and try and tease out more details about him.

Eveline's hope was that by the end of the day, they would start to see Roger's history and get a more rounded sense of his identity. Hopefully, they'd also be able to fill in some of the gaps in Roger's timeline over the days leading up to his death.

Abby didn't love the plan, but she had to admit that she did indeed have Christmas gifts she still needed to buy. And if all that was on the cards was Jane's nosiness, then she didn't see what harm it would do. Maybe they could find something out that gave them a clue about what happened to Roger, or maybe they just got more information that helped, but either way, it seemed the most unobtrusive way to take a couple of steps forward.

Giving the okay, they got ready to head out. Abby invited Luke, but he apparently had better things to do, as all teenage boys everywhere did when their mums asked them to go shopping. They were all going to split up, Abby would shop, Jane would gossip and Eveline would be sitting in a café ready to take notes.

As Abby purchased her fourth gift of the day, she received a phone call from Lisa.

"What are you guys up to today?" Lisa asked.

Abby wasn't quite sure how to answer. Should she admit that Eveline and Jane were out talking to people, trying to get more of an idea about Roger and his movements in the run up to his death? Abby chose to tell a half truth, and admitted to being in Folkesdowne catching up on her Christmas shopping.

"I've been thinking," Lisa started. "I know it's dangerous and I know DI Murphy warned us off, but I've decided I want to see this through."

"Eveline and Jane will be so pleased," Abby said, wondering how Jane's informal interviews were going.

"Do you think they'll be annoyed at me?" Lisa asked, concerned they'd think she was messing them around.

"Oh, I'm pretty sure they'll be absolutely fine." Abby knew she had to tell the truth. "They may actually be using the list you and Clarissa gave us, talking to some of them right now."

"Really?" Lisa sounded pleasantly surprised, much to Abby's relief. "Are you meeting up with them once you're done with your shopping?"

"I am."

"Would you mind if I joined you?"

"Sure."

"And beforehand, I might nip into Roger's office, see if anyone has anything of note to say about him."

"Even better. I'm meeting them at three. We're going to have coffee and cake before tonight's event."

"Great, see you at 3."

Abby texted Eveline to let her know the update, and to expect Lisa.

"I'm sorry guys, Roger's office was closed so I've got nothing new to add I'm afraid." Lisa hadn't even sat down before she shared her news. Abby almost wished she hadn't told her about what they'd been up to today, she felt like she was about to disappoint her even more.

"Same," Jane said. "Today was a total bust for us too."

"Oh no," Lisa eased herself down into the empty chair, a smile plastered on her face but Abby could see it was just a front. "So what do we do now?"

"We just keep working at the threads," Eveline said. "Something will come loose, it always does."

Abby had to wonder how true that was though. She remembered reading a statistic online some time ago that stated that about 20% of all murders in the UK remained unsolved each year, so those threads obviously hadn't come loose, and instead had remained tight and impervious. What if Roger's murder was one of those 20%? Putting herself in Lisa's shoes, Abby wasn't sure how she'd ever get closure on her friend's death if the case remained open. And what about his poor daughter?

"You never know," Jane said, in an obvious attempt to lift the mood. "We might strike lucky at the event night. You just don't know when a clue will show itself."

Chapter Twenty-Three

The event that night was being held at the local refugee centre. Everyone was made welcome by the centre manager, who introduced some of the refugees. "We have Iranians, Iraqis and Albanians here. They all fled their homelands in search of a better way of life, in search of peace and safety, something that we here in the UK take for granted. We invite you to come and chat to us, try the food made right here at the centre, and learn a little about different cultures and why these people risked so much to come to this wonderful little country of ours."

Abby was keen to immerse herself in tonight's event. Feeling like she'd led a sheltered life, she realized she'd never even met an Iranian or an Iraqi, and knew nothing about their culture. The closest she'd come was trying persian food, which she'd thoroughly enjoyed.

Persian traditional music was played quietly in the background creating an intimate ambience. Drums were dotted around the centre's ground outside with fires burning inside them to keep people warm as they mingled.

Abby noticed a number of locals grouped together in the corner, cautiously watching. She wondered whether they were just shy or, like her, hadn't had much exposure to other cultures before. She watched as a man walked over to them and engaged them in conversation. It wasn't long before he had them chatting animatedly with a couple of younger refugees.

Jane brought Abby over a persian tea, which Abby held in both hands, using it as a hand warmer to guard against the incoming frost.

"I've just met a wonderful young man," Jane said. "A doctor as well. Bit young for you though." And with that useful bit of information, she flitted away again, off to find more interesting people to chat to.

"Charming!" Abby said. She caught sight of Hilary as she weaved in and out amongst the growing throng of visitors, all curious to find out what went on inside the refugee centre.

Hilary paused her intricate weaving dance just long enough to say hi to Abby and Jane and offer up some respite for the night. "You might as well get in there and mingle Abby. Looks like tonight's door is a bit of a social event, eh?"

"Lovely," Abby said. She headed straight over to a table where she could see pots of food and people standing around eating something that was making Abby's mouth water. The smell was divine, a heady scent of spice with the earthy smell of the burning wood from the fires. As Abby tucked into some harissa chicken stew, which she learned was a very popular dish to eat around this time of year, she could see Lisa coming towards her, waving her hand and diving around people in her haste to get to her.

"You have got to come with me," Lisa said, animatedly.

"What's up?" Abby asked. She was in no mood to move when she'd found the perfect spot to rest her bowl of stew and her second cup of persian tea.

"I've found someone who remembered seeing Roxie with Roger, flirting."

"Well, we know all about that," Abby agreed, still standing her ground.

"We know about the fight on day five," Lisa said. "But did you know that Roxie was also flirting with Roger at the circus school?"

"Really?" Abby was intrigued now. She worked the timeline back in her head, trying to remember when the circus school door was.

"It was day seven," Lisa said.

"Oh," and then "ooh!" as Abby realized that meant poor Lance was made a fool of again. "Did Lance know?"

"I don't know. But I think it's a bit suspicious that neither of them said anything."

"Well, quite," Abby agreed.

"What are you two chatting about?" Eveline asked as she and Jane strolled over. Jane had a paper plate with some type of dessert on it.

"Don't even bother asking for one," she warned, her hand guarding the goodies on the plate.

"What are they?" Abby asked, shovelling the last forkful of harissa chicken into her mouth while she waited for Jane's answer.

"They're bamieh, like little doughnut sticks, but so much tastier."

"Ladies," Lisa interrupted, almost bursting with

excitement at the news she'd uncovered. She told Jane and Eveline what she'd just been telling Abby.

"Oh, we must go and meet the person," Eveline decided.

Jane was busy looking around.

"Jane, are you coming?" Eveline asked, wanting to go and quiz the witness.

"I swear I saw Roxanne here before," Jane said, searching the faces of those close by.

"Oh, this just got interesting," Eveline announced, a grin spreading across her face.

Lisa led them over to the other side of the grounds, where she had spoken to the woman who had attended the circus school advent door event. En route though, Eveline almost bumped into Roxanne, who was distractedly looking down at her phone.

"Oh, hi," Roxanne said.

Eveline jumped straight into questioning mode. "So glad we bumped into you, Roxanne."

"Really?"

"Yes. We were just told that you were seen at the circus event, flirting with Roger."

Abby cringed at Eveline's directness but Eveline seemed pleased at Roxanne's flustered reaction.

"I don't know what you mean," Roxanne said, looking frantically around.

"We don't want to put you on the spot," Abby took over, hating the panicked expression that had taken hold of Roxanne's face, which Abby assumed could mean Lance was here too.

"I wasn't flirting with him," Roxanne said, defending herself.

"That's not what we heard," Eveline said, cutting in with a sharpness that made Abby, and Roxanne, uncomfortable.

"I was chatting to him, that's all," Roxanne admitted.

"Can you tell us about what?" Abby asked.

"Just about the fight with Lance. I wanted to make sure he was alright."

"And was he?" asked Abby.

"Well, he asked me to meet in the pub after the event for a drink. So I would say yes, he was good."

"Weren't you worried about Lance finding out again, though?" asked Abby.

"I guess. A bit. I didn't really think about it. It was just a friendly chat."

"Was it? Could it be something else, like the thrill of the chase maybe?" asked Abby. She could see that what she'd suggested hit home with Roxanne, as colour started to flush into her cheeks.

"I guess maybe, a bit."

"I know some people thrive on the thrill of getting caught too?" said Abby.

Roxanne grimaced. "Roger is just…"

"Just what?" Lance had appeared, standing next to Jane.

"How long have you been there?" Roxanne asked, her voice becoming shrill as nerves got the better of her.

"Long enough," Lance said. His face was contorted in a pained expression and Abby found she was holding her breath, waiting for an explosive reaction.

Lance didn't explode though. He simply walked away. Head bowed, shoulders slumped. Abby wanted to run after him, offer some kind words or something, but hesitated.

Roxanne, on the other hand, did not. "Thanks!" She spat out the words forcefully before running after Lance, calling out his name. Lance didn't turn around though, and when Roxanne caught up to him he didn't slow either.

"Maybe he'll finally see the light and dump that girl for good," Eveline said.

"Eveline!" Abby snapped. "You could be kinder."

Eveline shrugged. She felt like she was too old to pussyfoot around someone else's feelings, just to spare them from the inevitable.

Lisa wasn't sure what to do after seeing the fall out of the confrontation with Roxanne. She wasn't sure whether she should even introduce the woman who had seen Roxanne now, which seemed almost like a moot point.

But Eveline had other ideas. "Did that woman you meet say anything about Lance being there on circus night?"

"Not that I recall. I didn't really ask about whether Lance was there or not," Lisa admitted.

"Shall we go and find out then?" suggested Eveline. She was keen to get a fuller picture of what had happened that night.

And by the time they had finished talking to the woman, Dierdre, they were all glad they hadn't left it as unnecessary.

Dierdre told a completely different version of that night's events. Apparently, Dierdre saw Roxanne on the stage area, trying out the ground-level tightrope. Dierdre had remembered Roxanne because she'd been so impressed with how she'd walked the line so gracefully, without a single wobble.

"That woman was a natural born circus performer," Dierdre said. "She was mesmerizing to watch. But then in walks a man, who I now know to be Roger. He's walking past the stage area, and the woman stops and waves. She went from this confident, in control woman to this needy one, playing up for attention. When he waved back but continued walking, she jumped off the tightrope. I mean, when I say I jumped off it, it wasn't high, just above ground level so people could practice on it."

"So it's Roxanne who approaches Roger then?" Eveline asked, confirming what Dierdre is telling them.

"Yes, unless it wasn't their first encounter that night. Anyway, I'm intrigued so I watch as she runs over to him. They seemed to be having a heated discussion for a few minutes, it was very intimate, a lot of touching. She leaned in a couple of times but he backed away. I remember it so clearly because I was surprised by it."

"Would you say that it was Roxanne who tried to initiate any intimate contact then?" Eveline enquired.

"I'd say so, yes. But I just want to stress, this is all just my impression of the event. I couldn't hear anything, so it was just the way I read their body language."

"Completely understood," Eveline reassured Dierdre.

"Thank you so much," Lisa said.

As Dierdre moved away, wanting to rejoin her group, Abby and Jane came in close, almost creating a circle.

"What do we think?" asked Lisa.

"I think Roxanne has a bit more explaining to do, don't you?" Eveline stated, matter of factly.

Chapter Twenty-Four

The next day, Lisa, invigorated by the revelations of the night before, decided to head over to the accountancy firm again where Roger had worked. Her plan was to ingratiate herself with whoever ran the office, and see if she could get any office gossip.

The office was based in a commercial building in town. It was a four storey Victorian building, located not far from the High Street. There was a small area behind the office with space for cars and a little seating area in the centre, with seating built in around an old oak tree. Being the last building in a row of similar structures, the accountancy firm seemed to have secured the best location, right beside a stream, where Lisa stopped for a few minutes to admire the view and watch the ducks gliding past.

Entering the main door, Lisa was met by a beautiful Christmas tree, taking pride of place in the lobby. At the side was a long desk area. A security guard sat behind one of the desks, reading a book.

Lisa was directed up to the third floor via the lift at the end of the lobby. From the signage behind the reception desk, she noticed four different companies shared the building, with Mercury Accounting taking up the third floor.

The lift opened up into a wide, open lobby space. Lisa's eyes were immediately drawn to the desk set right opposite the lift. A gonk sat on the top of it, with a small Christmas tree to the side. Nowhere near as grand as the decorations in the main lobby downstairs, Lisa noted.

There was no-one behind the desk so she hung around, waiting for someone to appear. She didn't have to wait long before she spotted a woman approaching from a door to the left.

"Oh, hi there," the woman said. "Sorry, I hope you haven't been waiting long?"

"I just got here actually," Lisa said.

"Can I help you? I'm afraid I'm the only one here today, so I'm afraid I may not be who you're after."

"Actually, I've not come to see anyone in particular," said Lisa. "I'm a friend of Roger's."

"Oh, poor Roger. Dreadful news that was. I couldn't believe it when I heard what happened." The woman offered Lisa a seat on the sofa set against one of the walls. "Can I get you something? I was just about to make tea if you'd like one."

Lisa accepted the offer of the tea. She may as well see if the woman had anything to share, and it seemed she definitely wasn't going to get it from anyone else at the company that day.

The woman, who introduced herself as Vera before going to make the tea, had explained that most of the accountants worked from home during the holidays so she usually had the place to herself.

"Don't you ever get lonely, or fed up, here by yourself while they're all at home?" Lisa asked. She was pretty sure that she'd begrudge having to come in if everyone else was able to stay home.

"I don't mind it actually," Vera said. "I like having the place to myself. And Bob, the boss, is fairly relaxed. He doesn't mind what I do here as long as someone's manning the desk.

Vera stood up and moved back around to her desk, disappearing behind it for a few minutes before reappearing with a half-knitted Christmas sweater. "I keep myself busy, see."

"Oh wow, I love that," said Lisa, genuinely amazed at the detail. "I wish I could do something as creative as that."

They chatted for a few more minutes before Lisa brought the conversation back around to Roger. Now that she'd warmed Vera up, she was pretty sure she could get her to open up on any office gossip. And open up she did.

Chapter Twenty-Five

Day 16: The Square

"I'm sorry," Abby said. "She said what now?"

Lisa had left the accountancy office in a state of shock, calling Abby as soon as she had let the door close behind her. Twenty minutes later she was sat in Abby's kitchen, bringing Abby, Jane and Eveline up to speed on her visit to Roger's former place of work.

"He was a randy old devil, wasn't he?" Jane said, almost impressed.

"So let me get this straight," said Eveline, still trying to wrap her head around the news. "Not only was Roger having affairs with Roxie and Jenny, but he was also having a fling with the boss's wife?"

"That's what Vera said. Apparently they'd been at it for years behind Bob's back."

"What, and he didn't know?" Eveline asked, incredulous.

"Seems not to have, according to Vera. They kept it

very hush-hush apparently."

"Wow!" Jane was slightly in awe of the man.

"But, I mean, it could be that Bob found out?" Abby speculated. "So potentially, we could have ourselves a whole new suspect."

"Well exactly!" Eveline agreed. "So I guess the only thing to do now is to find out where we can bump into this Bob character, and go and have a word."

"I might have the answer to that too," Lisa said, proudly.

"Oh, you go girl," Jane held her hand up in the air, palm open, waiting for a high five, which Lisa excitedly delivered.

After confirming with the golf club that Bob would be teeing off at 8am the next morning, Lisa and Abby headed out to the advent event. Eveline and Jane had decided to skip the night and settle in for a cosy night indoors. They'd already convinced Luke to pick them up a Chinese takeaway from the local Chinese and had a movie set up to play on Luke's return.

The event was back at the square tonight, where Hilary was helping to set up various tables with foldable chairs. The local youth club had helped to arrange the event for day sixteen, and had recruited some of their teenagers to help out. Abby wandered amongst the tables to see lots of different activities set up. There was pin the nose on the snowman, crazy can alley with fluffy snowballs, hook the snowman hat and snowball toss. Teenagers manned each of the games with others sitting at the tables where Christmas colouring pages and Santa letter templates were piled up, ready for the children to colour or fill them in.

Abby sat at the Santa letter table, picking up one of the templates. It was sectioned out. First Santa wanted the name and age so he knew who had written the letter. Next, he wanted to know whether the child had been naughty or nice, he even asked the writer to list three kind things they'd done that year so he could see exactly how good they'd been. The letter finished with a section to write in what you wished for. The little template brought back so many memories of when Luke and Will were young and Abby used to go all out for Christmas, trying to make it magical for them.

As the visitors made their way into the square. Abby gave them the lowdown of what was happening and where they could head to. Members of the creative team were milling around in colourful Christmas jumpers, encouraging the children to try out all the activities.

The cafe in the square had agreed to stay open late so people could get hot drinks and gingerbread cookies and one of the volunteers did a hot chocolate run, dropping a delicious whipped cream extravaganza into Abby's hand as he passed.

Christmas music played over a speaker that had been set up in the square and, looking around, it almost felt like Abby was in a Christmas market of sorts or slap bang in the middle of one of those cheesy Christmas movies she binged on throughout the month of December.

After thirty minutes, one of the elves took to the middle of the square, microphone in hand. This was Abby's cue to move into position, a sort of human perimeter fence appearing around the square as the elf made his announcement. "Boys and girls, mums and dads, ladies and gentlemen, as you've been enjoying the activities laid on tonight with the help of the Bank Youth Club you may have seen candy canes dotted around. If you have, then you've got the upper hand because right now, we need to get ready for the candy cane hunt."

Everyone started looking around, and a couple of the kids even peeked under the tables to see if they could spot anything on the ground.

"When I say go, the hunt begins. The aim is for everybody to get a candy cane so if you have one spare feel free to share. Okay, let's begin the countdown. Three, two, one...go!" And to the happy squeal of excited kids, the hunt began.

The human barrier made sure no children could escape the confines of the square in case there were any runners. Any children who didn't enjoy running around could sit and write their letter to Santa or take advantage of the near-empty activity stations.

Chapter Twenty-Six

Eveline and Jane were up bright and early the next morning, eager to meet with Bob and find out if he knew about his wife's affair. Jane knocked on Abby's bedroom door at 7am with a cup of tea as a sign of appeasement for the early start. Abby dragged herself out of bed and into her en suite, splashing water on her face to wash away the last vestiges of sleepiness. She was definitely not an early bird, one of the numerous reasons she'd found a flexible job she could do at home as the thought and practicalities of being a single mum, heading out to work early and not getting back until teatime wasn't something Abby had wanted to do anymore.

The golf course was in an idyllic setting, not too far from Folkesdowne. The views all around were awe-inspiring. Being positioned on an elevated plot of land, looking out onto the lush, green countryside, spending time in such soul-restoring views Abby could see the appeal.

They'd apparently already missed Bob when they

enquired after him. It was suggested that he'd only be on hole two or three so they could go out and find him if it was urgent. They decided to wait in the restaurant until Bob was done. The temptation of a full English breakfast was far greater than the idea of walking a golf course, and potentially getting hit by a ball.

So while Bob played his nine holes, his regular early morning course for the winter months, Abby, Lisa, Eveline and Jane tucked into fried bacon, sausages, beans, grilled tomatoes, baked beans, fried mushrooms and black pudding, with toast on the side.

Bob appeared as they were relaxing in the lounge, stomachs full to bursting, drinking more coffee.

"I hear you've been waiting for me, ladies," Bob drawled as he approached the table. He pulled a chair from a nearby table, plonking himself down in it and looking quizzically from one to the other, his hands steeped, chin resting on his fingertips.

Eveline took charge. "We just have a couple of questions if you don't mind, about Roger."

"That clown," Bob scoffed.

Eveline scowled at him, thinking it the height of rudeness to speak ill of the dead.

Bob shrugged, sitting back in his seat, waiting for a question.

Eveline decided to take the upper hand and ignore his outburst. "We believe he worked for you?"

"He did. But you should probably know that I was going to fire him this week."

"Just before Christmas?" Jane asked, shocked.

"Absolutely. The man had dodgy dealings going on. He was about to drag my company through the mud, and I wasn't about to let that happen."

"Is there any truth to the rumour that he was also

having a relationship with your wife?" Lisa asked, wanting to steer the conversation around to Roger's long list of flings.

Bob laughed. "And why would that bother me?" he asked, a cruel glint in his eye, or so Abby thought. But maybe the cruel glint was more her interpretation of his answer.

"She is your wife?" Jane pointed out, making Abby smile as she realised she wasn't the only one irritated by the man's attitude.

"Maybe on paper, but we haven't been a happily married couple for quite some time. And I couldn't care less if she had an affair with that waster. More fool her."

Abby glanced over at Lisa, conscious that the derision spilling from Bob's mouth would be having a negative impact on her, and she would be right. Lisa's jaw was tight, her eyes bore down on Bob with an intensity Abby knew found its root in hate.

"If you're not bothered about him sleeping with you wife, do you have an alibi for the night Roger was murdered?" Eveline asked. She knew that before too long the conversation was going to descend into chaos if he continued spouting his impressions of Roger about.

"You know, you women come in here, into my sanctuary, asking me questions about this man and his relationship with my wife, and now you have the audacity to ask me if I killed him?"

"I didn't ask that, Bob," Eveline replied calmly. "I asked whether you had an alibi so you can be ruled out as a suspect. This is a usual question given you've expressed pretty strong feelings about Roger."

"Have you shown me an ID card?" Bob challenged. "Are you lot even from the police, you certainly don't look it?"

"We never said we were from the police, we only said we had some questions," Eveline answered.

"Well if you're not from the police, I have no obligation to answer any more of your questions, do I?"

"You don't," Eveline admitted.

"Then I think we're done here, don't you?"

"One more question, if I may?" Eveline asked.

Bob didn't answer, but he also didn't stand, which Eveline took to mean he was open to answering it.

"You said you were going to fire Roger?"

"I did."

"May I ask on what grounds?"

"I found out he'd been cooking the books for one of the clients he'd brought in. If you want to look at someone murdering Roger, I'd focus less on his many women friends and more on his business dealings. And speak to Francesca Swenson, she owns Swenson Designs, some interior design company or such. It was her and Roger who were trying to give my business a bad reputation."

"Thank you," Eveline said. He may have been gruff and unapproachable, but Eveline was wise enough to realise he had helped a great deal in opening another line of inquiry on the potential reasons for Roger's death.

Bob stood, gave a curt nod of his head by way of goodbye and left them to it, moving through to the restaurant area where his golf buddies were waiting for him.

"I didn't like him," Jane announced as soon as he'd left the room.

"Me neither," Abby and Lisa both replied in unison.

"It doesn't matter whether we liked him or not," Eveline pointed out. "The man just blew our investigation wide open."

"How so?" Lisa asked.

"Did you know Roger was cooking the books?" Eveline asked.

"No, but then I'm not sure I believe he was, just because that loathsome man said so doesn't mean it's true," Lisa answered.

"But he gave us a name to support his claim. So we seek this Francesca Swenson out, we find out whether there's any truth to Bob's claims."

Eveline made sense, as much as Abby hadn't liked Bob, she had to admit that he had given them a potentially vital clue. "Okay, so how do we go about finding this Francesca woman?"

"I think we have to go by the company, see if we can seek her out that way," Eveline said.

While Abby drove them all home, Lisa jumped on her phone and googled Swenson Designs. Francesca had a shop on one of the little roads off the High Street, close by the accountancy firm. Deciding to drive by and hopefully speak to Francesca that day, they were thrilled to find the shop open and a woman sitting at a desk, as they went inside. The woman was organizing fabric swatches into colour after a customer had rifled through them, leaving them an un-coordinated mess.

"Francesca?" Lisa asked, tentatively.

The woman looked up. "Sorry, no. Francesca is out of town on a business trip. She'll be back in the office around midday tomorrow. Is there anything I can do to help?"

"No, thank you. It's Francesca we wanted to speak with. We'll come back tomorrow afternoon, if that's okay?"

"Of course," the woman answered, turning her attention back to the fabric swatches.

THE ADVENT MURDER

Chapter Twenty-Seven

Day 17: The Sports Centre

With plans in place to stalk Francesca's office the next day, everyone agreed that a night at the advent event followed by dinner and a drink at the pub was in order. Luke was out with friends and Will wasn't due back for a couple more days so Abby welcomed the girls' night.

They were at the sports centre tonight, using the big hall for an activity event. That was all Abby knew until she walked into the room. It had been sectioned off. First, there was a curtain that divided the room in two, usually used so two different clubs could share the space for different classes. Tonight though, the curtain was to separate one activity from the other.

On one side of the room, eight Christmas trees were positioned, each in their own marked out square. Next to each tree was a box full of Christmas decorations. The point of this, Abby learned, was for families to compete against each other in friendly head-to-heads. Eight families or groups of two to five would start, getting five minutes each to decorate their tree. The winners of each round would then compete against each other to be crowned 'Best Tree Decorator in Town'.

On the other side of the hall, huge polystyrene balls were laid out, in varying sizes. Hilary took great pride in telling them about the rules of the game. Again, each family or small group, would get five minutes to build a snowman using the polystyrene balls, before they were then allowed to delve into the box of snowman attire to dress the snowman. To make the snowman competition more challenging, buckets full of fake snowballs lined the edges of the snowman squares so spectators could try and hit the polystyrene snowmen down before the contestants had had a chance to dress them. Any left standing where then judged, and similar to the Christmas tree competition, winners of each round would then be pitted against each other in a snowman building showdown.

"Oh, this sounds like so much fun!" Jane said excitedly when Hilary had finished explaining the rules.

"Well, that's great news," Hilary said. "Because I have a favour to ask."

"Fire away," Eveline said.

"I was wondering whether you'd both like to be judges for the snowman competition?" Hilary looked at Eveline and Jane pleadingly, before backing away and running over to the corner of the room. "Wait," she called out, routing around in one of the many bags that were lined along the edge of the room. She pulled out two clipboards and lifted them up into the air. "I have these to make it more official."

"We would have said yes without the official merch," Eveline said, reaching for the blue clipboard as Hilary made her way back to them.

"Yes, we would," Jane agreed. "But don't we look fantastic with these?" She posed with her pen poised to write on the piece of paper that was clipped to the board.

"Okay, great. Thank you ladies," Hilary said, whisking Jane and Eveline away to rundown how she wanted the competition to be judged, and the contestant details recorded.

Abby saw Lisa come in and smiled as she noted Lisa's surprise at the way the hall had been laid out. Spotting Abby, Lisa ambled over. "I can't believe how different it looks in here," she said. "I usually play football in here. It's just, wow!"

While Hilary finished explaining their roles to Jane and Eveline, Abby walked Lisa through the rules for both games.

"What do you think?" Hilary asked, walking back over to Abby and Lisa.

"I love it," Lisa gushed. "It's going to be so much fun tonight. How did you even think up this idea?"

"Well, the sports centre were keen to get people in who maybe wouldn't normally come, so they could see that sport could just be about having fun and moving around, so we came up with this craziness."

There was some noise from outside the room, indicating that people were starting to arrive. Quickly explaining their roles to Abby and Lisa, Hilary then headed over to the team, making sure everything was ready.

"I'm going to be shattered by the end of this," Abby said, half joking. Their role was to un-decorate the trees ready for the next rounds, and Abby was not exactly looking forward to that part of the role.

Lisa's shocked face was similar to every other adult's

when they walked through the doors, wondering what was in store. The excitement on the kids' faces as they came in was thrilling. To see all the little faces light up as they saw all the Christmas trees made Abby well up a little.

All of a sudden she wished her boys were there to share in the fun. When she saw Luke walk through the door with his friends Abby had to stop herself from running over and hugging him, but when Will followed him in she couldn't help but leave her spot and half-walk, half-run over to get a cuddle.

"What on earth are you doing here?" Abby asked when she'd composed herself a bit.

"Surprise!" Will said.

"I can't believe you," Abby said. "And your brother knew you were coming home and didn't tell me?" Abby looked over at Luke, who smiled sheepishly.

"We wanted to come and see what has kept you busy for the whole month," said Luke.

"Well, you guys have come on the perfect night," Abby said.

After explaining what was going on and what her job was for the night, the boys offered to be tree un-decorator helpers., much to Abby's delight. Now, instead of just Abby and Lisa trying to dismantle the decorations on eight trees, they now had four strapping teenagers to help. Abby could feel herself almost glowing with happiness and pride.

And one round in of the Christmas tree decorating competition, Abby was feeling massive relief that the boys had showed up. The noise in the hall was insane, as spectators lined the sides checking on the families as tinsel and baubles flew through the air in a mad dash to create the most festive looking tree.

Over on the other side of the hall, Jane and Eveline were in their element. They had Jeff helping to dismantle the snowmen when the round had finished, alongside a couple of other local volunteers. Jane and Eveline were having so much fun barking orders at the crowd to pummel the contestants' snowmen as they tried to race to the finish line. While the volunteers dismantled the snowmen after each round, Jane had even drafted in some pre-teens to be on ball duty. As soon as the whistle was blown – Jane's favourite part of the job – the pre-teens would run all around their side of the hall, collecting the fake snowballs and filling the buckets back up so there were plenty available for the next round.

The way Jane and Eveline were running the show, it wasn't clear what part of the action was the favourite part for the crowd, as the whole experience was proving so popular.

With both sides nearing eight rounds of each game, the atmosphere was electric as the finals took place. Rather than play the finals at the same time though, the curtain separating the two sides was drawn and the whole hall got to watch both finals.

First up was the Christmas tree final. As Hilary blew the whistle to start, Abby and Lisa walked around the contestant areas as they got busy with their decorating duties.

As Abby walked past one of the small groups participating, she heard one of the men shouting out instructions to one of the women. "Shirl, come in, what is with you this week? Get in the game, babe."

Abby looked over at the woman she was guessing was Shirl. Her body language was off, like she didn't want to be part of any of it. Abby felt sorry for her, recognising herself and her own inhibitions in this woman, who was obviously not enjoying the spotlight.

"Are you okay?" Abby quietly asked the woman, trying not to draw any attention from anyone else.

The woman nodded, resigned to her fate as her partner basked in his five minutes of fame.

"Yes!" the man shouted, as they finished their tree just before the whistle was blow to indicate the end of the final round.

As the Christmas tree judges walked around, assessing the quality of the decorating jobs, Abby hung close to the couple, equally keen to see their reactions if they won or if they didn't.

The man did not disappoint. On hearing that they came a close second to a family with three pre-teen kids, the man grabbed some tinsel from the tree and threw it back in the basket. "Thanks Shirl," he said as he walked past the woman, blaming her for their loss.

The victors were ecstatic, especially the kids, pumping the air to cheers from the crowd. Abby watched as the little faces changed from excitement to pride. The cheering audience made the kids' day, and Abby could well imagine this night being a topic of conversation around the dinner table for some time. There was a battle over who got to hold the Christmas Decorator trophy, but the youngest of the kids won out in the end, much to Abby's amusement.

Next up was the snowman dressing final. Hilary was letting Jane and Eveline run this final, seeing as they were such a big hit with the crowd, and they didn't disappoint as Jane walked out into the centre of the hall, shouting, "Who's ready to rumble? And whose snowman will take a tumble?"

Abby laughed. She'd missed their antics as snowmen judges so far, but she wasn't surprised that they'd turned the event into the highlight of the night. Eveline rallied the ball collectors together, giving them a few words of encouragement for their final round and as the contestants took their places. Jane blew hard on the whistle, starting her stopwatch.

Chaos descended as the groups in the final snowmen competition frantically tried to build and dress their snowmen as the spectators tried to knock the snowmen down with the fake snowballs. As soon as the snowmen were built a flurry of snowballs would fly through the air, trying to make contact with a snowman head.

Some groups tried to fight back against the snowball onslaught, grabbing the snowballs off the floor and chucking them back at the spectators. Others designated one of their team to act as snowmen bodyguards, guarding the snowmen at all times, batting away the flying snowballs, as the rest of the group tried to dress him.

After what seemed like far longer than five minutes, Jane blew the whistle, shouting out, " We have a winner!" in a booming celebratory voice.

A dad with three boys was pumping the air, high five-ing his sons as they all congratulated each other on the win.

As the trophy prize was handed out, Eveline wandered past Abby. "Eardrums still intact?" she asked, sarcastically.

"That was crazy," Abby said.

"I mean, who's bright idea was it to give Miss Lordypants there a whistle?" Eveline asked, pointing at Jane, who was very much still enjoying her fifteen minutes of local fame.

Chapter Twenty-Eight

After the excitement of the evening, Lisa tried to cry off going to the pub.

"That took it out of me, that one," Lisa said.

"I know what you mean," Abby sympathised, feeling a bit drained herself. The boys had disappeared into the night, staying just long enough to see the finals before promising Abby they'd be home by 10pm.

"Do you mind if I skip the pub, I just don't quite feel up to it?"

As Abby went to respond, Eveline beat her to it. "Is it that you're tired or is it just too much happy feelings when you feel like you shouldn't be feeling happy at all?"

"Eveline!" Abby scolded.

"I don't mean it in a mean way," Eveline said. "I just wanted to say, sometimes when we're grieving someone we loved, it can feel wrong to have good days, like you're betraying them in some way."

"It is a bit of that," Lisa admitted.

"And that's completely understandable," Eveline said. "And it's been no time at all, so your feeling are your feelings, and you are allowed to feel whatever you want and need to feel. Just know, it's okay to feel the good ones too. It doesn't mean you loved them less, or don't miss them anymore."

Lisa smiled appreciatively. It had felt weird, when she'd realised she'd been enjoying herself. And then, she'd felt guilt. And then anger, at herself, and at everyone else, for acting so normally when the world should just be quieter and more solemn.

"Go take a nice bath, and be kind to yourself," Eveline instructed.

"Yes Mum," Lisa said, nodding.

Jane persuaded Eveline and Abby to go for a drink at the pub, still too pumped up to go home. They found a table by the entrance, so they could people watch, and Abby was surprised when she saw the woman from the Christmas tree decorating competition walk in with a woman Abby didn't recognise from earlier. The two women grabbed drinks at the bar before finding their own table, directly behind where Abby was sitting.

"Oh, she was at the event tonight," Abby said casually, pointing the woman out to Jane and Eveline.

"Did she win?" Jane asked.

Abby shook her head.

"Probably drowning her sorrows then," Jane decided.

Abby chuckled. "Well, given how her other half reacted, she probably is."

"How did her other half react?" Eveline asked, never skipping an interesting tidbit.

"Had a toddler huff," Abby explained. "But instead of throwing his toys out of the his pram, he threw the tinsel in the bin."

Jane laughed, while Eveline rolled her eyes, amused by people getting so competitive over a silly competition.

Abby suddenly touched her lips with her index finger as she tried to sit back to better hear the conversation happening behind her.

"Roger would never have behaved that way," the woman who Abby had seen at that night's event was saying.

Abby looked across at both Jane and Eveline, to see if they'd picked up on what she'd just heard, but neither of them could hear the conversation over the rowdy pub noise.

Abby whispered the woman's words.

"Another one?" Jane said, her left eyebrow raising in surprise.

As Jane and Eveline sat quietly while Abby continued to eavesdrop, every so often Abby would lean forward to catch them up on the latest snippet of conversation. "Apparently, she's sick of being taken for granted, by Darren."

"Must be the husband," Jane decided.

"She's sad about what has happened, but feels like she can't grieve properly cos she was having an affair."

"That's harsh," Eveline agreed.

"Wow, I mean, how was Roger managing all this?" Jane felt like she had to ask. The man seemed to have enough stamina to keep half of the town's female population interested."

"I just don't see how he had the time," Abby said, feeling exhausted just thinking about the amount of juggling he must have had to do.

"What was the husband like?" Darren?" Eveline asked. She was wondering whether they had another name to add to their suspect pool.

Abby thought back, though she couldn't really remember much about him, other than he was competitive, and a sore loser. "It's a shame Lisa isn't here, she seems to know half the town. She might have known who we were dealing with."

"Do we ask right now?" Jane wondered.

Abby turned around, but immediately turned back again as she witnessed the woman crying into her friend's open arms.

"Whoever this Roger was, he certainly left an impact didn't he?" Eveline noted.

Chapter Twenty-Nine

"Did she say anything about the Darren character from last night?" Abby hadn't even walked back into the kitchen before Eveline started in with the questions.

"She's not sure she knows him. Maybe if she'd been there she might have recognized his face but," Abby shrugged. It felt like another dead end, like a light shining through a doorway only to be extinguished as you edged closer.

"So what now?" Jane asked.

Abby wasn't sure what to suggest and hoped Eveline had some good ideas, but Eveline was too busy using Abby's milk frother to contribute anything meaningful to the conversation. "Maybe we head back to the office and see if Francesca Swenson is back in town yet?"

"What about Bob's wife?" Having poured the now frothy milk on top of her coffee, Eveline took a sip of the hot drink, smacking her lips together. "Delicious."

"How would we even find out where Bob lives?"

"The secretary. They know everything about everyone, especially the boss." Jane said.

"Is it maybe time we split up?" Eveline suggested. "Me and Jane could tackle the secretary and go and pay a visit to Mrs Bob, and you could drag Lisa over to the office and camp out there until this Francesca character turns up."

While the idea to go back to the office had been hers, Abby wasn't sure she wanted to take point on the task, and her hesitancy must have been evident in her facial expression as Jane walked over and gave her an encouraging pat on the back. "You'll be absolutely fine, I have every faith in you."

"I wish I shared your confidence," Abby mumbled, suddenly feeling self-conscious.

As Jane retrieved their coats Eveline gulped down her coffee, fuel for the upcoming run-around. "I know it feels a bit scary doing this on your own, being in charge, but you've got this Abby. Jane isn't wrong."

Abby sighed. She hated confrontation at the best of times, didn't even like making phone calls and would put them off if at all possible. Heaven knows how she'd got this far in life, but here she was. "Time to put my big girl pants on then," she said ruefully, seeing Jane and Eveline out of the door.

She'd called Lisa as soon as they'd left and convinced her to meet at the office in an hour. Abby had had to use the promise of a hot chocolate as a bribe to get Lisa to accompany her but felt immediately happier that she'd have an accomplice.

They met on the high street and nipped into the Cinnamon Café for a fully loaded hot chocolate, whipped cream oozing out and slithering down the colourful mugs as Abby grabbed an empty table looking out onto the street. Abby loved the bustle of Christmas, everyone seemed happier and the early onset of darkness made for cozier rendezvous. It was almost like you could smell Christmas in the air, the scent of pine needles from the spruce trees lingering and competing with the cinnamon smells emanating from the coffee counter.

Lisa was still at the counter, and Abby watched as she chatted with the man behind the till. She wondered whether they were in a relationship or just friends, there was definitely a level of intimacy there that Abby found she was feeling jealous of. Lisa turned, noticing Abby watching them and gave a quick wave before turning back to the man and blowing him a kiss. She walked over to the table Abby had managed to nab, her hands holding two small plates, the contents of which Abby couldn't quite see.

"Here you go," Lisa placed one of the plates in front of Abby and watched, amused, as Abby's eyes widened. The biggest, most delectable-looking piece of chocolate cake was taking up most of the plate, a scoop of vanilla bean ice cream to the side.

"Wow, that looks amazing," Abby licked her lips in anticipation, gratefully accepting the spoon from Lisa's hand. "So, who's the guy?" she asked between mouthfuls.

Lisa looked over, as if she didn't know who Abby was talking about. "That's Joe."

"And Joe is?" Abby wasn't letting her leave it at that.

"Oh shoot" Lisa said, her head nudging Abby's attention to the window.

Abby glanced out the window and then looked again. DI Murphy was glaring at them, an icy stare that somehow seemed to fit in with the paper snowflakes that hung from the tops of the window frames.

"What have we done now?" Abby wondered, sitting

up straight in her chair. DI Murphy made her way through the door of the café and took a direct route over to the table Abby and Lisa were sitting at.

"Ladies," DI Murphy said.

"Hi," Abby answered, trying not to let any feeling of subservience show through.

"I trust you ladies are just having coffee, and not planning on how to get in the middle of my investigation, are you?"

"Of course not," Lisa said, smiling calmly.

Abby stayed quiet. She wasn't good at lying, and found if you couldn't trust your words, you were best stopping them from coming out.

"Where are the older two?" DI Murphy asked, casting a quick look around the café.

Lisa looked at Abby, who was still trying to control her tongue from blabbing the truth. "They're back at Abby's," Lisa said.

DI Murphy looked from one to the other, but having no evidence of wrongdoing she gave them one last warning glare before walking over to the coffee counter.

"Cat got your tongue?" Lisa asked as soon as the policewoman was out of earshot.

"Sorry, I think I've got a truth problem with authority figures," Abby said.

"In your line of work?" Lisa sounded sceptical.

"Do you want to leave our plans for today?" Abby was now feeling sheepish and wondering whether she needed Eveline and Jane by her side to be able to do this investigating schtick. Not for the first time did she wonder whether maybe she wasn't cut out for this type of work.

"No," Lisa said. "We're here now, we may as well do what we'd planned.

"But what if we bump into DI Murphy again? What if she actually catches us at the offices?"

"Then we say we were picking up some bits for Roger's daughter. We can just blag it."

.

It turned out that Abby needn't have bothered worrying, the office visit was a bust. They managed to chat with the secretary again but Francesca Swenson was nowhere to be seen and the offices had been empty other than the solitary woman. The only thing they'd come away with was a company brochure, a smiling picture of Francesca Swenson on the back cover, looking like the epitome of success and glamour. Looking very much like the woman who was currently exiting the very building Abby and Lisa had just left.

They'd been standing on the other side of the street, across the road from the Swenson Design offices. Abby had been returning a call from Will and Lisa had been standing to the side, looking through the window design of the gift shop and giving Abby some privacy, when Abby had noticed the door to the offices open. Her interest piqued, she watched to see who would come out and was a little taken aback when she recognized the woman as being the same one as the photo on the back cover of the company brochure.

"What a liar!" Lisa was saying.

"She was there all along," Abby said. "Do you think she knew we were there, looking for her?"

"Of course she must have. She must have told her secretary not to let anyone through," Lisa guessed. "What do we do now, confront her?"

"Not yet. Let's follow her, see where she goes."

Abby told Will she'd see him at home and ended her call, pulling her gloves back on and tucking the phone back inside her front coat pocket. Not for the first time did she silently congratulate herself for choosing a winter coat with pockets big enough to hold her phone and gloves.

Ready for a long evening of following Francesca to wherever she was off to, both Lisa and Abby were pleasantly surprised when Francesca stopped only two streets away at a cosy wine bar called Frank's. They decided to follow Francesca in and hover at a nearby table to see if she was meeting up with anyone but when they went inside the bar was busy and the only vacant seats were up at the bar, right next to the woman herself.

She'd ordered a glass of chardonnay and as the waiter set the glass down in front of her, Francesca thanked him and then turned to Abby and Lisa, "Do you two want a drink?" she asked casually.

Abby was a little taken aback. She'd assumed Francesca hadn't noticed them following her. Maybe she wasn't as good at this spying game as she'd thought she was. She heard Lisa ask the bartender for a chardonnay and mumbled that she'd have the same, her brain still trying to catch up and work out how to play the next few minutes.

"I hear you've been hounding my secretary?" Francesca said.

It wasn't that Francesca had an intimidating frame, but she was obviously a woman who knew how to play hardball. You could tell just by looking at her and the way her chin jutted out, her head held high and shoulders down and set back, looking completely relaxed and in her element.

Abby tried to mimic her body language by straightening her back and pulling her shoulders down from around her ears. It felt unnatural, her usual posture being more curved and crouchy, but she was determined she was going to walk away from this conversation with her self-respect intact. "We're trying to find out what happened to Roger? We've been led to believe that you were a client of his?"

"Oh dear," Francesca almost purred her answer. "You two aren't more of Roger's scorned women gang are you? You know there's a fair few of you." She laughed, amused.

"He was my friend," Lisa said. "We weren't in a romantic relationship."

"Oh, poor you," Francesca's tone was sickly sweet but Abby could hear the condescension beneath it. "I heard he was rather good in bed, seems you may have missed out."

"Did you?" Abby challenged, incensed by Francesca's flippant attitude.

"Most definitely not. He serviced his clients very well, bells and whistles, the lot. Very good at his job, was our Roger."

Abby glanced over at Lisa, who looked like she was having a hard time keeping it together. "And which part was he best at then, gigolo or money launderer?"

"I beg your pardon," Francesca said, her voice becoming instantly hostile. "You ladies want to be careful. I could sue you for libel, sullying my good name like that."

"So Roger wasn't cooking the books for you? Putting through interior design jobs that didn't exist? Making your business appear ten times more profitable than it was?"

"And why on earth would he do that?"

"Oh I don't know," Abby teased. "Maybe to keep your investors happy? I imagine they wouldn't be best pleased if they knew how poorly you were really doing?"

Abby watched as Francesca's face turned a shade of red that almost matched the red silk scarf she wore around her neck. "How dare you?" she said, her tone low as she looked around to see if any of the regulars were paying attention.

"We just have a few questions if we may." Now that Abby had made it clear that they knew about Roger's extracurricular activities, she was keen to know if there was anything else they could learn.

Francesca Swenson was having no more though. Without another word, she pushed the stool back, causing it to scrape angrily against the stone floor, and made for the door, leaving her glass of wine untouched.

Abby wondered whether they should follow her again, but Lisa had other ideas. She finished off her own glass of wine before reaching across for Francesca's untouched one. "That went well," she said as Abby watched her body visibly relax and shake off the encounter.

Chapter Thirty

Jane greeted Abby and Lisa back at the house with a warm smile and the promise of gossip and goodies. Sure enough, as they walked through to the back of the house, the smells of winter spices filled Abby's nostrils. Eveline was busy pouring mulled wine into four mugs and as she set the cups down on the kitchen island she turned back and bent down to retrieve a tray of warm mince pies from the oven.

"Oh wow, have you two been shopping again?" Abby asked.

"Bob lives in a gorgeous little village not far from here," Eveline explained. "These are from the delicatessen there. We got chatting to the woman who owned it."

"Of course you did," Abby couldn't help but comment.

"His house is amazing," Eveline continued, ignoring the interruption. "It's an old Kent Oast House with one of those circular towers, just dreamy."

"His wife is lovely too," Jane added.

Eveline pulled a face, the corners of her mouth turning down.

"You don't think so?" Abby asked, picking up on Eveline's nonverbal message.

"She was too jittery. It made me wonder whether she knew something she perhaps wasn't supposed to," Eveline followed up.

"So does this mean Bob is back on the suspect list?" Abby asked.

"I think he has to be," Eveline said.

Abby took a bite out of the mince pie that had been calling out her name. The pastry had just the right amount of texture, a perfect companion to the fruity mincemeat, the spiced undertones setting off a little dance party on her tongue. She washed it down with a long sip of mulled wine, savouring the heat and letting it warm her up from within.

Suddenly feeling nostalgic for a time before she spent her spare time solving crime, Abby had to remind herself of why they were looking into the untimely death of Roger. "We found Francesca Swenson."

"Really?" Eveline seemed impressed. "And?"

"And she was horrible," Lisa answered.

"She was a bit of a bully," Abby agreed, smiling encouragingly at Lisa.

"I don't care about her character, dear," Eveline said. "What was your feeling about her possible role in Roger's demise? Could she be a potential suspect?"

Abby wasn't sure how to answer. Sure, the woman was rude but if every rude person was also capable of murder there'd be hardly anyone left in the world, or so Abby thought.

"Did she act guilty in any way?" Eveline tried a different prompt.

"She didn't like that we knew about the cooking of the books," Abby said.

"They never do," Eveline replied. "So what is your gut telling you?"

"Honestly?" Abby's hand subconsciously travelled to her stomach, moving in a circular motion as if the movement would prompt a gut response. None was forthcoming though.

"All I can say is that it felt like we could have got more out of her, if she hadn't run away that is."

"Well, that's encouraging," Eveline said.

"Is it?" Lisa asked. "I mean she might have just been covering the fact that she was having some dodgy dealings. It might just be that."

"It might be," Eveline agreed. "But the point is it wasn't a dead end. There's a lead and if there's a lead we can follow it, right?"

"Follow it where?" Lisa asked.

"Well, only time will tell," Eveline answered cryptically. "Is there anything else to share?"

"We got told off again," Abby said. "DI Murphy caught us in the café, warned us off again."

"Did she now?" Eveline said. "I wonder whether it's time we found out how much DI Murphy knows about the business side of things."

"I could give her a call," Lisa offered. "I have her number."

Lisa moved away from the table and into the hallway, to make the call, wanting a bit of quiet while she spoke to the policewoman. "I don't suppose anyone fancies a trip to the movies, do they?" she asked as she came back into the kitchen.

Jane had been catching Abby up on Bob's wife, Marjory, but stopped talking as soon as Lisa came back in with her question. "You know, I can't remember the last time we went to the movies, Eveline."

"Why on earth the movies?" Eveline asked.

Abby reckoned she knew why. "Isn't that the advent door for tonight? A Christmas showing at the local cinema?"

"It is indeed," Lisa said, giving Abby a cheesy thumbs up.

"I still don't get what that has to do with our policewoman," Eveline said. "Surely she's not going to the movies in the middle of an active investigation?"

"Surely you should know better than most that the police are allowed to maintain social lives throughout their varied careers, Eveline?" Abby shot back.

Eveline tutted, making Abby wonder if Eveline had ever taken time off from work. "I was just getting comfy with my hot wine and mince pies," she grumbled.

"Oh, come on Eveline," Jane said. "It'll be fun. And it'll kill two birds with one stone."

Chapter Thirty-One

Day 18: The Cinema

Eveline was still grumbling about having to brave the outdoors again when they rounded the corner to the cinema. It was just off the high street in Folkesdowne, a throwback to the days when all types of entertainment establishments could be found in town, easy access to people in the surrounding areas without a car. Nowadays it was more of an inconvenience, having to pay hefty parking charges at the in-town car parks rather than take advantage of the out-of-town sprawling entertainment and shopping complexes that the newer cinema chains could be found at.

The old Edwardian building housed the local museum too, with the library a mere stone's throw away. All had seen better days Abby was sure, but she was grateful that such amenities still existed, however little they were now used. She was ashamed to admit that she hadn't stepped foot in a museum since the boys were younger, and made a promise to herself to try out all of these free activities as soon as the Christmas season was over.

There was no sign of DI Murphy but the cinema doors were open so they all wandered inside, hoping they'd catch her in the foyer. They lingered there for ten minutes, but as the announcement to take seats came over the intercom Abby grabbed some popcorn and other snacks from the kiosk and joined the others as they made their way through to the auditorium.

The lights were dimmed a little for ambience, but were still bright enough so you could make out empty seats. They spotted a row of four empty chairs six rows from the front so made a beeline for those. It was only when they were seated that Abby allowed herself to look around.

They were seated in the stalls but Abby looked admiringly at the balcony seats, which looked much more appealing with framed portraits of film stars from film's heyday framing each balcony alcove. The red velvet seats echoed the red of the walls, making Abby feel like she was in a 1950s film studio. If it wasn't for the flickering neon lights from the children's toys that kept catching her eye, she could have easily imagined herself having time-travelled to a bygone time.

It felt good to be on the audience side of the Christmas calendar events for a change, and Abby waved as one of the volunteers she recognised from the other events waved at her.

"I've found her," Eveline announced satisfactorily. No revelling in the moment for Eveline, Abby mused as she followed the direction Eveline's finger was pointing in. It took a few seconds for Abby's eyes to zero in on DI Murphy, who was standing in the second row, chatting to some people milling about in the aisle.

"Do we go and nab her now, do you think?" The words came out but as soon as they did Abby realised they were too late as the auditorium lights dimmed further. "Never mind," she muttered.

Instead, she settled into her chair to enjoy the Christmas movie The Snowman, tucking into her popcorn as the film took her back to Christmases past. It finished to a round of applause, as someone dressed in a snowman costume walked onto the stage at the front and thanked everyone for coming to see his show.

Parents with little ones queued at the front to get pictures with the snowman and Abby stood, her eyes back on DI Murphy, trying to predict which exit she was going to use. It was difficult to keep up with her though, and with people in the row of chairs wanting to leave, they ended up being pushed along with the crowd towards the foyer.

Abby, Eveline and Lisa waited in the corner of the foyer, hemmed in by the passing crowd, looking out for the detective. Jane could be seen on the other side of the foyer, chatting animatedly to one of the volunteers who was also trying to direct the crowd towards the exit and hand out flyers for the upcoming events at the cinema.

"You lot waiting for me?" DI Murphy appeared at Abby's side, a twinkle of mischief in her eyes.

Abby nodded.

"What did you think of the event?" DI Murphy asked.

A little surprised by the unusual friendly tone, Abby responded before Eveline interrupted, ever the professional.

"We wanted to give you a bit of an update," Eveline said.

"Really? Usually it's the other way around you know,"

the detective grimaced as someone's bag smacked into her back. "We should probably take this outside, out of the way."

Chapter Thirty-Two

They'd reconvened in the bar two doors down from the cinema, all the cafes having closed. Lisa and Jane headed to the bar to get a round of gluhweins while Abby and Eveline filled DI Murphy in.

The policewoman was tight-lipped as Abby explained how they found out about Roger's accountancy antics. They talked about their conversation with Bob, about his wife's affair and his anger at discovering Roger's illegal dealings with Swenson Designs and Francesca Swenson's hand in it all. DI Murphy tried to hide her surprise but Abby could see from the way her pupils contracted and expanded that some of what they were sharing was new information. She didn't expect the policewoman to admit that she wasn't aware of any of this, but at the end of their story DI Murphy leaned back against the back of the stool, digesting the details. "That's quite a bit to take in," she said. Abby couldn't tell whether it was the whole story or part of the story that DI Murphy hadn't been privy to, and DI Murphy wasn't about to reveal all her cards. Instead, she thanked them for the information and made her way out of the bar.

Lisa and Jane put the drinks down on the table just as DI Murphy's back could be seen moving out into the street. "Was it something we said?" Lisa asked, wondering what she should do with the spare gluhwein.

"I think she might be going to do something about everything we've just told her, maybe," Abby gratefully took the glass of gluhwein, her fingers caressing the embossed glass design of the glass and she raised it to her mouth, the winter spice aroma filling her nostrils as the warm, red wine hit the back of her throat. "That is so good."

"There's a spare if you want it," Lisa said, holding up the drink she'd bought for DI Murphy.

"So what part of the story didn't she know?" Jane asked.

"She didn't say," Abby said.

Eveline had an idea though. "I'm guessing the affair part wouldn't have come as a surprise, but if Marjory is right and Bob's work is front and centre of everything he does, you've got to wonder whether he kept the part about Roger's business antics to himself. The last thing he'll want is to have his business dragged through the mud."

"Shall we pop in on Marjory in the morning?" Jane asked, anxious to make sure her potential new friend was okay. "I could call her, let her know."

Abby nodded, it all seemed to fit. If he wasn't bothered about his wife having an affair though, she wondered whether that meant he was having his own, or was he just not a relationship type of guy. She'd certainly met her fair share of those, men who talked a good game but in the end put their work above all else. Technically, she was dating one. James would be quite happy being single for the rest of his life, or so she'd bet.

The next morning, Abby was up early, nursing a bit of a hangover from the gluhweins. She'd guzzled down the spare and then they'd all had another, seemingly forgetting that the soothing liquid contained a serious amount of alcohol. And red wine gave Abby the worst kind of hangovers, so much so that she couldn't even stomach a cup of tea that morning, and was instead trying to add an injection of vitamins into her body with a fruit smoothie.

She'd had just enough energy to grab some coconut water from the fridge and add it to the blender with a banana, some ginger and some of the pineapple chunks she'd bought for Luke the other day. Thirty seconds of blasting it while nursing her sore head and Jane found her sitting on the small sofa in the kitchen, hands wrapped around the glass delicately supping her hangover cure.

"You only had three," Jane said, looking disappointed.

Abby made her excuses before joining Jane at the kitchen island, bringing her sherpa blanket with her. Wrapping it around her shoulders before resuming her position of nursing her smoothie in both hands, Abby watched as Jane busied herself frying bacon and buttering rolls while setting the teapot on the island.

"This will sort you out," Jane said, placing a bacon roll in front of Abby before walking out into the hallway to call Eveline and the boys down for breakfast.

Abby's eyes were drawn to the fridge where the advent door calendar was taking pride of place. It had the locations of each door written down, and tonight it was at the old Village Hall in the older part of Folkesdowne, before it became the bustling town it was today.

It was December 19th, and the door for the evening was a Christmas jumper fashion show. It would be only a few days until Christmas Day itself, and Abby wondered whether they'd still be investigating Roger's murder on Christmas Day, and did that mean she would be hosting Jane and Eveline throughout the Christmas holiday.

Dawning on her that the Christmas shopping pre-order she was scheduled to pick up from the supermarket in two days wouldn't feed them all, Abby wondered whether Jane and Eveline would be staying for Christmas now. And then what about Lisa, Abby mused.

She'd only just met the woman a couple of weeks ago, but she found herself worrying about how she was going to spend Christmas day. Thinking about it, she didn't really know too much about Lisa, other than the fact that she'd lost one of her best friends right before Christmas, and that she lived in Folkesdowne. Abby realised she didn't even know if she was married or had kids, how could she not know that?

Jane came back into the kitchen, and set five mugs on the island, pouring in the tea from the teapot before adding milks and sugar and setting the cups out on their designated places. As Eveline and the boys made their way into the room, Jane directed them to their seats by pointing to their specific mugs of tea: milk with one sugar for Eveline, milk and two for Will and his sweet tooth and just milk for Luke, who liked it exactly like his mum did, strong and hot.

"We still up for visiting Marjory this morning?" Jane asked once everyone was happily tucking into breakfast.

"Definitely. I want to find out if DI Murphy has been

in touch yet after what we told her last night. She might know whether Bob has been approached again or not," Eveline said.

"Imagine your husband caring more about his business than he does about you," Abby said, finding herself comparing her story to Marjory's again. "Did they have kids?"

"I don't think so," Jane said.

"The woman must have been so lonely. No wonder she ended up succumbing to Roger's charms," Abby looked across at her boys. "I hope you two make better husbands than that horrible man."

Luke groaned, rolling his eyes and looking at Will. Will paid no heed though, grabbing his second bason roll and heading out of the kitchen, followed closely by Jane who wanted a bit of privacy while she phoned Marjory.

Chapter Thirty-Three

Day 19: Fashion Show

"She didn't sound too good on the phone," Jane said, as they pulled up in front of a house Abby didn't recognise. Abby had to stop herself from commenting as she'd heard the same statement at least four times since Jane had finished her call with Marjory.

Eveline was the first to approach the front door, ringing the doorbell as she waited for the other two to catch up. Abby pressed the lock button on her car keys as she leaned up against the wall adjacent to the front door, waiting for someone to answer.

A minute had passed before Eveline banged on the front door again. "Marjory, we know you're in there," she shouted through the letterbox.

"How do you know she's in there?" Abby asked, seeing no signs of anyone being at home.

"That's her car," Eveline pointed to a silver Porsche

Cayenne parked in front of a double door garage at the side of the barn conversion.

Abby stepped back from the front door and looked up, admiring the stonework of the 19th century oast house. She'd always coveted the Kentish oast houses since the time she'd moved down to this part of the UK. If she was honest, it was the conical roofs that drew her attention, though the idea of filling out a round room with furniture wasn't something Abby thought herself capable of doing with any real flair.

The front door jerked open and a dishevelled woman, who appeared to be in her late 50s, appeared in the doorway. She was wearing a pale green dressing gown and was holding a large wine glass filled to the brim with wine.

"What do you want?" the woman slurred.

"Marjory," Jane stepped forward. "Remember us dear? I called you this morning."

"Oh right, yes," Marjory backed up, opening the front door fully, which Eveline took as an invite to enter the house.

The first thing Abby noticed when she walked through the door was the pile of clothes lying at the bottom of the stairs. Bob wouldn't be happy on his return, given they looked to be his.

"Bob not here?" Eveline asked, eyeing the pile of crumpled suits.

"The police came to visit him this morning but he was at his golf club, as usual," Marjory said, her words slurred.

It was a little after 11am and Marjory was already slurring her words.

"Why don't we get you a nice cup of tea?" Jane asked, leading Marjory towards the kitchen.

Abby could hear Marjory protesting as she was led

away down the hallway. Not sure whether to follow or give Marjory and Jane some space, Abby hung back. She noticed that Eveline had done the same.

"Do you think she's going to be okay?" Abby asked, feeling unsure of what her next step should be.

Eveline didn't answer, distracted by something. "Can you hear something?"

Abby lifted her left ear to the ceiling, listening out for whatever Eveline may have picked up. Sure enough, there was some kind of constant noise, like a tap running or overflowing maybe. "I think it's coming from upstairs."

"Be a dear and go and check it out, would you?"

"I can't just go wandering around upstairs," Abby protested, though as she said it she did wonder whether there was anyone else in the house. If not, then soon enough the water would be trickling through the ceiling, and she didn't want to be the person who could have prevented that from happening.

Eveline said nothing, but gave Abby a pointed look.

"Fine!" Abby said, taking two stairs at a time as she rushed up to the first floor to find out where the source of the running water was coming from.

The first door she opened was to a lavishly decorated bedroom, which Abby assumed to be the master suite. She didn't have the nerve to walk through it to check whether the running water was coming from the ensuite preferring to leave that option to the end when she'd checked everything else off. Rummaging around upstairs was one thing, but Abby felt like invading Marjory's bedroom was maybe a little too much.

Instead she carried on, trying a couple more doors before finally coming across the main bathroom, which thankfully was the source of the water. It appeared that Marjory had been about to take a bath when we'd disturbed her. And looking around the bathroom, Abby had to wonder whether it would have been a wise choice.

On the windowsill just above the bath was an opened bottle of champagne but it was what was beside the champagne that caused Abby the most concern. An opened pill bottle lay on its side, a few of the white pills had escaped and were laying on the windowsill soaking up the rays from the winter sun.

Chapter Thirty-Four

Abby picked the bottle up and turned it over, trying to work out what kind of pills it contained, but she had no idea what the typed words could mean. Alprazolam was a drug Abby hadn't heard of before. The one thing she was certain of though was that Marjory was far too intoxicated to be taking any type of medication.

Making sure the tap were off and pulling out the plug for the bath, Abby grabbed the champagne and the bottle of Alprazolam and made her way back to Eveline, who was still waiting in the hallway. "I'm not sure what these are, but this might be why Marjory seems so out of it?"

"Oh dear," Eveline grabbed the bottle from Abby's outstretched hand and turned towards the kitchen, making her way down the same hallway Jane and Marjory had disappeared down just minutes earlier.

Jane was at the kitchen sink, filling the kettle with water when Eveline and Abby walked into the kitchen. Abby couldn't help but take a moment to admire the room, which reached right to the top of the rafters, an airy room that felt almost church-like with it's huge windows and high ceilings. The kitchen itself didn't quite match the grandeur of its setting, looking like it hadn't been updated since the 80s, with a pine look to the cabinets and an old style aga taking up most of the back wall.

"Marjory," Eveline walked straight over to Marjory, standing only a metre away from her face as she looked down on her. "How many of these did you take?"

Marjory looked up at Eveline from her seated position at the kitchen table. Abby noticed how small she looked, sitting in the high-backed chair, slunked down, her upper body only just visible. "I don't know," Marjory said, her words slurred.

Eveline turned to Jane who had now put the kettle back in position and was watching the scene with interest. "I think we might need to call an ambulance."

"Really? You don't think she just needs to sleep it off, maybe?" Jane said, wondering what all the fuss was about. She'd mixed alcohol and tablets before, and while she knew it was frowned upon, she'd survived to tell the tale.

"This is a dangerous mix she's taken," Eveline said. "This is Xanax, do you know what would have likely happened if she'd have gotten into that bath?"

"She would have fallen asleep?"

"Potentially," Eveline said. "And maybe drowned?"

Jane remained unconvinced by Eveline's concern. Abby was starting to wonder whether Eveline might be onto something though, as Marjory was slipping so far down the seat she was going to be sitting on the floor any minute now. "Maybe Eveline has a point?" Abby said.

"Thank you," Eveline said. "Now who's going to phone the ambulance?"

Jane pulled out her phone, still wondering whether they were over-reacting or not. Assuming it was better to be safe than sorry, she dialled 999 and waited for the call to connect with an operator.

Meanwhile, Abby walked over to the table and tried to help Marjory from slipping any more. "Maybe we should move her to a couch?" she suggested.

Grabbing one side of Marjory's body, Abby managed to manoeuvre Marjory's body into a half-standing position, allowing Eveline to grab the other side and lift her to her feet. "Just let me sleep," Marjory said, trying to extricate herself from Abby and Eveline's grip.

They were so focused on trying to move Marjory that nobody heard the front door open and close, nor did they hear the footsteps making their way down the hallway and into the kitchen. It was only when Bob shouted, "What the heck is going on here?", his voice loud and gruff, did everyone turn to him, jumping as they did.

"Your wife has taken a some Xanax with alcohol," Eveline said.

"And?" Bob growled.

"It's a pretty lethal combination," Eveline explained.

"She'll be fine."

Jane waved her phone at that point. "I'm just on the phone to the ambulance service, they say they can get an ambulance out here in about ten minutes."

"Hang up that phone, she doesn't need a bloody ambulance, bunch of busybodies." Bob was standing in the doorway, surveying the scene in front of him. It had to be one of the worst ways to come home, watching as your wife was being manhandled by a group of women. Abby felt a little sympathy for the man, but his disregard for his wife's health was starting to aggravate her.

"Aren't you concerned about your wife?" Abby

challenged.

Bob snarled, before marching over to her and wrestling his wife's arm from her grasp. Marjory wavered on her feet, almost slithering down his body as a wave of drowsiness seemed to overtake her.

"You can see she isn't well," Eveline argued.

"Nothing a good sleep won't sort out," Bob said.

Jane was standing with the phone against her ear, still communicating with the operator on the other end of the line. "No, it's her husband," she was saying into the phone.

Bob let go of his wife's arm then, stomping over to Jane and grabbing the phone off her. "We don't need an ambulance here, cancel that request."

Abby could make out the faint plea from the operator to stay on the line before Bob ended the call. "You lot, get out of my house."

"Bob," Abby said, nervously stepping towards him. Eveline had managed to catch Marjory as Bob had let go of her, and had lowered her back into the chair.

"I don't know how many pills your wife has had," Eveline interjected, "but combining Xanax and alcohol is not a good idea. Look at your wife, Bob, does she look like she's in a fit state?"

Wondering why he was so against having an ambulance turn up outside his house, Abby tried a different suggestion. "Wouldn't it just be better to get her checked out, make sure she's okay? You're right, we could be over exaggerating, but we're just concerned. Knowing she was okay would sort this whole thing out, and then we will be out of your hair in a flash."

Bob's eyes narrowed in on Abby, and she could see his brain ticking over, though what was going on in there was a mystery.

"Do whatever you want, I want no part of this." And with that, Bob stormed out the way he came. Seconds later they heard the front door slam shut, and moments after that the purr of a car engine.

Abby followed him out of the kitchen just in time to see the car driving away, back down the driveway. She stayed at the front door for a minute, wondering what on earth he could be thinking. Why would he drive off and leave his wife in this state? And what did they do now, call the ambulance again? Or let her sleep and stay and watch her just in case anything untoward happened?

Abby was at a loss, unsure what to do. She didn't know how long she stood there for but as she was about to shut the front door she saw the neon yellow and orange of an ambulance as it approached the driveway.

Opening the door wider, she called out to Jane and Eveline, letting them know to expect some help. As the ambulance pulled up next to the front door, Abby moved out and took a couple of breaths of fresh air, clearing her head quickly before moving back inside to direct the ambulance man into the kitchen.

Chapter Thirty-Five

They'd followed the ambulance to the local hospital and had camped out in the waiting room until a doctor had come by to let them know that Marjory was in safe hands and would be staying the night at the hospital to rest up.

Abby had asked if they could see her but as they weren't family, the doctor had forbade it. Suggesting they come back the next day, Abby, Eveline and Jane had made their way back to the car.

"Where do you think Bob drove off to?" Jane wondered out loud.

"Who knows with that man," Eveline said as they stood at the parking machine, waiting for their turn to pay for the privilege of parking their car.

"Maybe he just couldn't handle the situation?" Abby said, wondering if that could be true. They moved forward as the couple who had been in front of them retrieved the receipt from the little slot and moved off, heading towards the far end of the car park. Abby dug inside her bag until her fingers touched up against the soft velvety feel of the purse Will and Luke had bought her for Christmas the year before.

"I think he might have just been ashamed," Jane said. "Imagine being confronted by your wife in that position. I mean, I wonder whether he felt any guilt about the way he's treated her for all these years."

"I'd bet you he wasn't even aware of how unhappy she was," Eveline wasn't giving an ounce of compassion to the man.

Having paid the fee, they wandered over to the car, none of them anxious to leave but knowing they had no business staying around either. Maybe Bob would visit in the night, Abby thought. Though how he'd know where she was troubled her. "Do you think we pop back to their house, see if he's back? I mean, how will he know where she is?"

"How about we just leave a message on their phone?" Eveline suggested. She was in no hurry to go back to that house and deal with the man for a second time that day.

"Do you have the number? Cos I certainly don't."

"I've got Marjory's mobile," Jane offered, "but I guess that's not much use."

"I don't want to go back there and help out that miserable man," Eveline said. "And anyway, don't you have an advent event to get ready for?"

"We can't go and be all jolly at a Christmas event when we've just checked someone in to hospital," Abby argued. "And we're not helping Bob out by telling him where his wife is, but we might be helping out Marjory."

"Abby's right, what if today was a cry for help and Bob actually turns up for once and provides the emotional support that poor woman needs?" Jane nudged Eveline out of the way to get to the passenger seat door, opening it with a smug look on her face.

Eveline tutted, relegated to the back seat. "Fine, let's go, but I'm not hanging around."

By the time they drove back up Marjory and Bob's driveway, the light was fading and barring the headlights leading the way, the front lawn was hidden by the dusk. It wasn't until they pulled the car around in front of the garage that they saw Bob, skulking by his car.

Abby pulled the car up in front of Bob's and hopped out. "Bob, I'm so glad we caught you," she stared.

But Bob was in no mood for small talk. "I know where she is," he says, without even looking up into Abby's face.

"Do you want to know how she is?" Abby tried again.

"I've spoken to the hospital. I'm going over there in the morning, I'm just getting some bits together to take over."

Eveline and Jane exited the car, distracting Bob's attention from Abby as they walked over. It gave Abby a chance to sneak a peek inside Bob's car. Spotting his golf bags taking up pride of place in the boot of his car, Abby looked closer. There didn't seem to be anything that looked like it belonged to Marjory inside the car. Maybe she was reading too much into it, Abby thought. It could just be that Marjory didn't have her own luggage, or maybe he was just a useless packer like her ex?

Bob noticed her eyeing up the car and moved into her line of sight, in an attempt to conceal the contents. "Look, I'm sorry, and I'm grateful that you ladies checked in on me and let me know about my poor Marjory, but I really must go. I've got so much to do."

"Like what?" Abby heard Eveline ask.

Bob stared at her, his demeanour becoming slightly combative. "I don't think I need to explain myself to you ladies, do you? Now if you wouldn't mind." He turned, trying to signal the end of the conversation with his body.

"You don't seem too bothered about your wife, Bob, if you don't mind me saying," Abby could sense something about the scene she was witnessing wasn't right, but she couldn't quite work out what it was.

"Listen, I've thanked you girls for coming over, I've explained that I know about my wife and her condition and that I'm going to visit her tomorrow, I don't really think anything else I am doing is really any of your business."

"Girls?" By the look on Jane's face Abby couldn't work out whether she was thrilled or offended to be called a girl in her seventies.

"Fine, ladies. But really, I must insist. This has been a bit of a day for me too, and I really need to just unwind and get some rest. You do understand, don't you?"

The chill in the air made Abby shiver and pull her coat closer to her body. She knew something was off with Bob, but she didn't know what. Really, what could they do? Barricade themselves to the house? Steal Bob's car keys so he couldn't drive away?

"Okay, well if you're sure everything's okay, we'll leave you to it. But we're planning on popping into the hospital tomorrow ourselves, to check on Marjory. We may see you there."

Bob stayed silent, but retreated back towards the house, giving a short, sharp wave as an acknowledgment that he'd heard what Abby had said.

As the front door closed behind him, Eveline turned towards Abby. "That was strange."

"Right," Abby agreed. "And if he's packing his car for the hospital visit tomorrow, why is he packing his golf clubs?"

"Because, dear," Jane said knowingly. "If he's anything like the men I used to know, he'll be going to the golf club first. Keeping up appearances and all that."

"Keeping up appearances?" Abby was shocked. "But his wife's in hospital, surely that looks bad even to that lot?"

"I assume he'll be trying to keep it quiet. Wouldn't want a sniff of scandal about now, would he?" Eveline clearly had the measure of the man.

"I'm a bit surprised he's not going over there now," Abby said.

"What, to the golf club?" Eveline asked. "It's a bit too dark for that now."

"No, to the hospital," Abby couldn't help but think of Marjory, a woman so obviously playing second or third fiddle in her marriage, and so evidently hurting because of it. Not only was she a work widow, but it appeared she was a golf widow too, Abby mused.

"Come on," Eveline tried to sound upbeat. "There's not much more we can do here, and I'm assuming you have another event tonight we have to get back for?"

Chapter Thirty-Six

Abby glanced at her watch, slightly panicked that she was letting people down, before realising she'd not been on the volunteer roster for that night's performance. It was due to take place in the village hall, but Abby wasn't sure she was in the mood for frivolity. "Mind if we just head home? I feel like I need an early night tonight."

"Wasn't it the fashion show tonight though?" Jane asked, her voice laced with disappointment.

Abby nodded, an image of her Christmas tree inspired jumper popping into her head. She'd been looking forward to walking the catwalk with her sparkly creation.

"You know I was going to win that competition, right?" Eveline said.

"You would not have!" Jane protested. "Mine was a marvel."

Maybe going out and letting off some steam was just what the doctor ordered, Abby thought, her mind coming around to the idea of attending. "Fine, let's go. But we'll need to go home first and get our jumpers.

Lisa was waiting for them at the village hall doors, resplendent in a sunny yellow jumper.

"I don't think you're going to win with that, dear," Jane said bluntly, looking Lisa up and down.

Lisa laughed, pulling her sweater down to show off the image of Santa in his red shorts and t-shirt, relaxing on a sun lounger. "You don't like it? It's Santa on holiday, December 26. I thought it was cool."

In response, Jane opened up her coat, giving Lisa a peek at her own Christmas-inspired jumper. "This is how you win Christmas."

Eveline playfully pushed Jane out of the way, beating her to the door. "Not if I've got anything to do with it," she said as she sauntered into the hall.

Abby chuckled, embracing Lisa in a big bear hug before joining the other two inside. She couldn't wait to tell Lisa about what they'd experienced that day, now convinced they had their suspect.

The hall had been decorated in bright reds and greens, tinsel festooned over every single possible orifice. At first glance, it looked gaudy, but as Abby's eyes got used to the décor, her feelings softened. Crazy decorations were absolutely in keeping with a crazy Christmas fashion show.

With no clue how she'd managed to pull it off, Abby congratulated Hilary on the catwalk, which was a raised platform with foldable seating along each side. It almost looked like an official fashion shoot, except for the array of wacky costumes, or maybe that made it even more authentic.

The fashion show started with the youngsters, all walking carefully down the raised platform, their little faces beaming with pride as they waved at the family members who were waiting their own turn to show off their flair for the festive.

The competition was split into age groups, with the under-13s winner being presented before a short contest for the teenagers, of which there were few. Abby wasn't surprised, she guessed street cred came into it, and the fact that this was a community event firstly and their parents were probably attending managed to keep most teenagers away.

The main fun started with the adults, who between them had decided to be as showy and extravagant as possible. Even Jane with her light-up bauble-laden jumper had competition. The women in the local knitting circle had evidently preparing for this day for months.

The event ended with a walk by all the volunteers who had helped out and Hilary, who received a big, deserved round of applause as she gave an embarrassed bow. Heading out of the door after an hour of pure fun, Abby linked her arm through Lisa's, filling her in on all that had happened that day.

They agreed to meet at the hospital the next morning, to check on Marjory but also see if there was any news on the Bill front. Abby wasn't convinced he was going to show up, and only time would tell.

Chapter Thirty-Seven

Day 20 – Improv Night

"Has her husband been in at all today?" Abby was asking the nurse as they all stood at the desk at the front of the hospital ward they were visiting. Lisa had met them at the front of the hospital, full of concern for Marjory, and some rather unsavoury rumours about her marriage to Bob.

Abby had woken to a last minute client request for some VA work so they'd had to delay visiting the hospital until the afternoon. Jane and Eveline had busied themselves in the kitchen, working on the corkboard they'd created with some pins Luke had had in a rub in his bedroom. They had pinched some thread from Abby's junk drawer and had been trying to add any missing details to the picture they were trying to come

Strictly speaking, they weren't really allowed to visit outside of visiting hours, but Marjory had a private room and the nurses at the station were feeling sorry for her as she hadn't had a visitor. Those two things combined meant they were able to sneak in, with strict instructions to keep it short.

As they walked into the private room, Marjory was awake and alert, her eyes brightening up when she saw familiar faces.

"How you doing?" Abby and Jane asked in unison, both moving forward and taking up positions close to the bed.

Marjory smiled sleepily. "Thank you for coming to see me. I was wondering if anyone was going to."

"Your husband hasn't been in yet?" Abby asked.

"Not yet, but he's very busy."

"He should be putting you first Marjory, especially on days like today," Jane had pulled one of the visitor chairs close to the bed and was sitting as close as she could get, holding Marjory's hand.

"He does, he's very caring behind closed doors." Maybe Marjory got to see a different side to her husband than Abby had seen, but she couldn't quite believe Marjory's words.

"Was he looking after you yesterday morning when we found you?" Abby could tell Eveline felt mean asking Marjory about Bob, but she was wondering the same thing herself.

"He was," Marjory smiled.

Abby stared at Marjory, convinced she'd misheard. "How was he looking after you yesterday Marjory?"

"He told me to take it easy, got me my pills and a glass of bubbly, said it would do me good to just have a bit of me time and relax. He even got me some special bath salts." Marjory smiled at the memory but Abby and Eveline weren't smiling at all. Even Jane was looking downcast.

"He gave you the pills?" Abby asked.

"And the fizz?" Eveline added.

Marjory looked at them, confusion in her eyes. "Well yes, he was making me feel better. I've had a wretched few days, not been myself at all."

"And he suggested a nice, warm bath?" Jane asked, her tone kinder than Abby's or Eveline's.

Marjory focused her attention on Jane, "Yes. He knows I like baths."

"Oh Marjory," Jane clutched the woman's hand tighter in her own.

Marjory seemed mystified by the quick change in atmosphere. Abby could tell she could sense something had happened, and Abby had to wonder whether her brain was purposefully not making the connections in a misguided attempt at self-protection.

Eveline sat on the edge of the bed, near the bottom. "He gave you the pills, Marjory," she said softly, making sure Marjory was listening. "And then he gave you the wine?"

Marjory nodded slowly.

"And it was Bob who suggested the bath after making sure you had had a cocktail of pills and alcohol? That doesn't sound like he was looking after you Marjory."

As realisation dawned, a white pallor spread across Marjory's face as her bottom lip wobbled. Jane leaned over to give her a hug. "I'm so sorry, Marjory."

Abby looked over Lisa, realising she'd been standing off to the side watching everything unfold. Stepping back to check she was okay, Abby touched her arm gently. "You okay?"

Lisa shrugged, her shoulders shuddering slightly as she did. Abby wasn't sure whether to stay standing next to

Lisa or move back closer to Marjory. Her heart hurt for these two women, their pain mingling together.

"What am I going to do?" Marjory was saying.

Abby had no answers. She'd not particularly liked Bob, but she didn't think him possible of trying to kill his wife. But was that what he had done? He'd certainly provided the alcohol and Marjory's prescription pills, but what would have happened if that was all Marjory had taken? Bob had intimated that Marjory had mixed her pills with wine before, but had she? Or was that a lie Bob had concocted to divert attention.

She needed to chat all this through with Eveline and Jane, needed to get the thoughts running around in her head down on paper so she could start making sense of what she was feeling. And more importantly, they needed to let DI Murphy know.

Chapter Thirty-Eight

Making their way through the hospital corridors, Abby couldn't help but wonder how Bob could have wanted his wife out of the picture. Yes, she'd had an affair and maybe that was it, maybe he'd felt she'd sullied his good name? But Abby wasn't convinced. Could a man be proud enough to want to an end the life of someone he'd felt had disrespected him?

"It's so sad," Jane was saying as she walked next to Abby. "I should have known something was up when I spoke to her yesterday morning. I told you she sounded off."

Abby remembered that comment, remembered being annoyed that Jane had continuously mentioned it on their way over to Marjory's house. And it was that that she kept tripping over.

It was still niggling on her brain as they walked over to the payment station in the car park. And it bothered her even more as she caught sight of Bob exiting his car. Without thinking, Abby quickly walked over to him.

Bob saw her coming and Abby could see him hesitate, checking out exit routes. "I only have one question, Bob," she said, as she stood in front of him.

His eyes wary, Abby ploughed on. "Did you give Marjory those pills and the alcohol yesterday morning?"

"Why would I do that? She's a grown woman, she can get her own."

"And did she? Get her own I mean?"

"How would I know? I'd left before she even got up that morning. And thanks to you lot, I've been in the police station all morning, being interrogated as if I was a mass murderer or something."

Abby had to concede that Bob looked shattered. "And Roger? You knew about the affair, or not?"

Bob shrugged. "I didn't care. It's not as if it's her first one."

"But why are you still together then?" Abby asked.

"Life was pretty good. I was out all the time, she could do whatever she wanted. We rarely spoke to each other to be fair, more like flatmates. And it was nice, getting home-cooked meals and being looked after when she wasn't busy with all her other things."

Turning around to try and catch the attention of the others, who Abby had to assume were waiting at the car, she was surprised to find them all standing right behind her.

"I'll call DI Murphy," Eveline said.

"Why?" Bob was looking at them, looking confused.

"Did you tell the policewoman about your wife's affairs?" Abby asked.

"I don't see what business that is of hers," Bob said.

"It might help her think less of you as a suspect?" Eveline suggested, scrolling through her contacts to find DI Murphy's number.

"I've told her, I'm not a suspect."

"Well someone killed Roger," Lisa said.

"And the husband of the woman he'd been having an affair with would be a prime suspect I'd imagine," Abby finished.

"You know, your wife was very happy to have us think you had purposefully fed her drugs and alcohol," Lisa said.

"No she wasn't," Bob said, hesitantly.

A car beeped behind them, the woman behind the wheel motioning for them to move out the way. The momentary distraction was enough for Bob to make a break for it, storming towards the hospital entrance.

Abby made off, trying to catch up with him. The others weren't far behind but none of them managed to stop him barging through the hospital reception and directly towards the ward where Marjory was staying. Abby had to wander how he knew exactly where to go, given she was under the impression that he had yet to visit. But he walked the route as if he'd been a hundred times before.

He walked straight past the nurse's station, waving at the nurse on duty. Did he know her? Abby wondered. He must, because they hadn't got far at all without being accosted by the on-duty staff as they'd entered the ward just the day before.

Watching as Bob marched into the private room Marjory was staying in, Abby held back. She wasn't sure whether she should be here for this bit, but then what if he got angry? Sidling up to the door, Abby peered through the little glass window of the door.

As Eveline, Jane and Lisa found their way to the room Abby raised a finger to her lips. "He's in there," she said, pointing to the room. "I'm not sure what's going on."

"Can you hear anything?" Eveline asked.

Abby shook her head. "Not really."

"Open the door just a smidge," Jane said, moving forward and manoeuvring her foot so the door slid open slightly.

They all huddled around it, straining to hear. Bob's voice came through loud and clear though. "You've played everyone, haven't you Marjory?"

There was no response from Marjory. Abby stood on her tiptoes to look through the little window again. Marjory was sitting up in bed, looking very smug, eating a yoghurt. "She looks fine," Abby said. "More than fine actually. Look."

Moving out of the way, Abby swapped places with Lisa first, before Eveline shoved her out of the way for a look.

"Those women you've got wrapped around your finger think the sun shines out of your..." Bob said.

Abby didn't hear about where the sun was shining from because at the moment an alarm rang out in the ward hallway, and the hallway erupted with activity as nurses and doctors descended on the ward the alarm had been triggered in.

Distracted by all the activity, Abby didn't notice Eveline growing more and more impatient. The next thing she knew Eveline was barging through the door, ready to confront the couple inside. Abby, Lisa and Jane were quick on her heels, if only to see what would be said.

"You lying toerag!" Eveline shouted, her anger directed at Marjory.

Chapter Thirty-Nine

Looking completely unaffected by Eveline's interruption, Marjory smiled sweetly. "Oh, you're here, so lovely of you to visit."

Eveline was having none of it though. "Lose the act, Marjory."

"Has someone not had their cup of tea this morning?" Marjory asked, her tone mocking.

"Bob didn't feed you the wine and pills, did he Marjory?" Abby asked, annoyed at Marjory's tone.

"I don't know what you're talking about," Marjory kept her tone sickly sweet, but Abby could see the flash of anger that crossed her face, her jaw tightening.

"You did that yourself. You knew we were coming and so what? You wanted us thinking Bob was a monster husband? For what purpose?"

"You don't know what it's like, do you? To always come second best to a job, a stupid game, to anything else but me," Marjory said.

"I gave you the world, Marjory," Bob said, his voice

quivering with anger. "And what did you give me? Never-ending abuse about how I wasn't giving you enough, being enough, doing enough. You know what? I've had enough."

"You gave me part of a world, Bob. But you always left me wanting more."

Wow, Abby thought. This woman was cold. "Why did you make us think he was so thoughtless though?" Abby couldn't get her head around why Marjory had acted so erratically.

Marjory shrugged. "Why not?"

"Because she needed us to think that Bob was cold. Because she needed us believing that he was capable of such callousness, isn't that right Marjory?" Eveline challenged.

"It was you, wasn't it?" Abby turned around to see Lisa visibly shaking. "You killed Roger." Lisa's voice cracked as she threw out the accusation, not giving Marjory time to respond before she rushed towards the bed, hand outstretched in an attempt to make contact with Marjory's face.

Abby grabbed at her coat, pulling Lisa away and pushing her back into the room. "That's not going to make anything better," she said, grabbing Lisa's hands in her own and making sure her face took up Lisa's attention, trying to refocus her.

A nurse popped her head around the door, "Sorry, but I can't have you all in here."

"Get them out," Marjory said, dropping her head into her hands.

"Don't pretend you're upset, Marjory. I know you're enjoying this," Bob said, a snarl on his face.

Marjory looked up, looking directly into Bob's eyes. Abby could see the hate lurking there, directed right at the man she'd apparently loved for all these years.

"Get them out!" Marjory screamed.

Bob stared her down. "You're a hateful cow!"

As the nurse tried to calm the situation and persuade them all to leave the room, DI Murphy entered. "What's going on in here?" She stood in the open doorway, two policemen behind her.

Chapter Forty

"Oh am I glad you're here. These women are harassing me," Marjory said, a tear pushed out of her left eye.

"She killed Roger," Lisa cried, extricating herself from Abby's hold and moving back towards the bed.

Marjory shrank against the pillows, "Please," she implored, "can you get them to leave?"

The nurse looked imploringly at the policewoman, silently calling for help. DI Murphy took her time, looking from one face to another, trying to read each one. Trying to get an idea of what she'd just walked in on.

Lisa started first, "She lied to us. She told us Bob had basically poisoned her."

"I told you nothing of the sort," Marjory said, her voice high.

"Well, you told us," Abby said, supporting Lisa's words.

Marjory sat tall in the bed, her face resolute.

Bob was having none of it though. Abby sensed he

was done with the charade of pretending to be happily married. And who could blame him if his wife had orchestrated her own hospital admission just to push blame onto him and make everyone suspicious of what else he could be capable of doing. "You're not pinning this one on me, Marjory. I didn't see you yesterday morning. And I certainly didn't give you any pills."

"She told us he did," Abby interjected so DI Murphy could follow the story.

"And I'm done with your affairs, your endless need to have all the attention," Bob continued. "If that Roger had any sense, he told you it was over. I know you don't like it when people tell you that, just look at the last bloke who tried to extricate himself from your grip."

Last bloke? Aby thought. She wasn't aware of any other men Marjory may have had a relationship with.

"She's got history, has our Marjory," Bob paused then, taking a deep breath, trying to steady himself.

DI Murphy took the opportunity to ask a question of her own. "Care to elaborate Marjory? These are pretty strong accusations being levelled at you."

"Yes, and they're all false." She looked at Bob, "And that sorry excuse of a man, you just can't keep it together, can you Bob?"

Bob laughed, but it wasn't a pleasant sound. It was a laugh filled with rage and disbelief. "It's exhausting being your husband. Why do you think I find so many distractions to keep me out of the house? And I don't mind all your indiscretions? It's a welcome break, at least it means some other poor mug has to deal with you."

"Because you're too weak to deal with women, Bob," Marjory spat. "You're pathetic."

Abby looked on in disbelief. Was this really the woman who she'd felt so sorry for the last few days, who'd painted a picture of the poor wife stuck at home, lamenting her husband. But a different story was coming out now, and Abby couldn't seem to take her eyes off the two main actors.

"So, are you admitting to having affairs, Marjory?" DI Murphy asked.

"I mean, wouldn't you? Putting up with this man, did you know we have separate bedrooms?"

Abby wasn't sure that was the insult Marjory had assumed it would be. She certainly wouldn't relish sharing a room with someone who thought so little of her.

"And was Roger one of those affairs?" the policewoman asked.

"Roger was weak too. He couldn't give me what I needed. And when I found out about the other women, who did he think he was? I'm not about to share a man."

"So, what did you do when you found out he was seeing other women?"

Abby had to give it to the policewoman. She seemed to be almost having a conversation, but one where, if Marjory wasn't careful, she was going to fall right into the trap.

"I confronted him of course."

"At the train station?" DI Murphy asked.

"Yes. He denied it of course, but he thinks women are stupid. Thinks they're play toys, things to have fun with and then discard. Onto the next. Well, I'm not going to be discarded by a man like that."

Abby hadn't noticed, but the nurse was still standing by the door, watching the scene unfold. She wondered how this would go down in the staff room later on, what they'd make of a patient being questioned in a hospital room. Abby had to wonder how many other patients had been interrogated like this, did it happen often, was it like on tv, or was this completely out of the ordinary?

"Did he tell you he'd give up the other women? Did you ask him to?" DI Murphy asked.

"He told me he would end them all, but then I came back out and find him chatting to one of his tarts again. Did he think I was stupid?"

"Who was he chatting to?"

"How am I supposed to know? Just some blonde."

"So what did you do Marjory? Did you hurt him?"

Marjory didn't answer. "I don't have to answer any more of your questions. I'm in a hospital bed, for heaven's sake, have some respect."

"It's answer them here, or we'll have to arrest you and do this down the station once you've been released." DI Murphy explained.

"Arrest me? For what?" Marjory looked at Bob. "Bob, are you going to allow this?"

"Marjory, look around you. You've basically just told a room full of people that you were having an affair with Roger. Not only that, you talked to him, and god knows what else, the night he was murdered. What did you do?"

For the first time that day Abby caught a glimpse of the Marjory she thought she'd recognised. She looked a little like a fox caught in the headlights, a realisation dawning that the game was up. "But, he provoked me. I didn't mean to hurt him, but he was so mean, so callous. He just threw me away, like a piece of chewing gum that got stuck to his shoe."

"He shouldn't have done that, Marjory, he shouldn't have hurt you like that," DI Murphy said.

Abby looked over at Lisa as soon as she heard DI Murphy's words, worried that Lisa was going to react in defence of her friend. She watched as Lisa's fist clenched at the side of her body, her jaw contracting as her eyes narrowed in on the woman in the bed. Abby moved closer to Lisa, touched her hand lightly, squeezed it with her own, ready to hold fast if Lisa tried to move again.

"I told him that, I told him he'd be sorry. Know what he did? He laughed. He just laughed at me."

DI Murphy was now at the edge of the bed, sitting in the chair next to it and leaning in, taking up the space around Marjory. She patted Marjory's hand. "Tell me what happened next."

It seemed almost like now that she'd started her story, Marjory had to get it out. "I hit him."

"With what?"

"I found some wood by the bins. I thought maybe I'd knock him out, but he wouldn't get up."

Abby seemed to step back to that night in her mind. She saw Marjory standing over Roger, it had been Marjory who had screamed.

"I panicked. Went back inside the station. I didn't know what else to do. I think I was waiting for him to come back in. But he didn't."

"How long did you go back inside for, Marjory?" DI Murphy asked.

"I don't know. Ten minutes maybe, twenty. I don't know. I couldn't think straight. I didn't kill him though, I only hit him. What I did, it couldn't kill a man."

Abby couldn't see Murphy's face, but she'd bet there wasn't a flicker of a reaction on it. "What happened next, when you went back outside?"

"I did, I went back out. I wanted to see if he was still there, still where I left him."

"And was he?"

"Yes, he hadn't moved. That's when I thought maybe he was dead, you know, maybe someone came and finished him off when he was down. That could have happened you know."

"What did you do with the wood?"

"What? Oh, that. When I went back, it was still there. And I thought, maybe it shouldn't be. So I threw it."

"Threw it where?"

"I don't remember, I just threw it."

"Oh Marjory," Bob moved to Marjory's side, stepping between his wife and DI Murphy. Marjory rested her head on his side, her hand holding the bottom of his polo shirt, weaving the errant thread that hung from the bottom between her fingers.

She didn't cry. Not one tear. Abby didn't know what to think of that. She almost looked relieved to have the story out. Maybe it was just the relief of not having to hold it in any longer.

DI Murphy broke the room up then, ordering everyone home, promising to check in with them all at some point over the day.

Chapter Forty-One

"What's going to happen to her?" Lisa asked.

They were back at Abby's house, all sitting around the kitchen island, mugs of steaming, hot tea in front of them as they tried to dissect what had happened.

DI Murphy had phoned to let Abby know they'd arrested Marjory and were charging her, with what though, Abby wasn't sure.

"Would it be murder?" Lisa asked.

"Maybe manslaughter? Abby suggested.

"It depends how much evidence they have, and whether they can prove the crime was pre-meditated or not. I don't know whether Marjory set out to kill him," Eveline tried to guess the potential outcome, knowing how tricky calling judgements could be.

"She might not have set out to kill him," Lisa said. "But it was the same result as if she had, his life was snuffed out. She has to pay for that."

"She will," Jane said, her voice full of feeling. "It just seems like such a waste. It wasn't really over anything after all, just a woman feeling belittled by a man. How many times does that happen in a day?"

"Too often, but women don't go around bashing the brains out of someone, do they?" Lisa argued.

There was little left to say. The day hung heavy on them, a conclusion they'd fought to get but one that left a bitter aftertaste. How could such sadness come from such a trivial event, a mocking.

Whatever had happened to make Marjory take that swing, to fight back like she had, to break with all reason so spectacularly, Abby could only guess at. Maybe they'd never really understand it, maybe they didn't need to.

Lisa had got her answer, the feeling of unknowing put to bed, but it seemed to do little to assuage the feelings of guilt of not being there. Grief was a tricky thing, knowing what happened helped, knowing the circumstances surrounding Roger's death made it a little easier to imagine, but getting past the pointlessness of the loss of life was going to take time.

Abby knew this. Knew this was just the start for Lisa, and there was a whole lot more misery still to come, but she hoped she could be a friend to help her through it. This investigating lark, it was hard. It took you to places you never really explored before, it made you look at people differently, open your eyes to what we all are capable of. Abby wondered whether anyone sitting around that kitchen island could be capable of it, capable of murder, and the short answer was, who knew.

The End

THE ADVENT MURDER

ABOUT THE AUTHOR

Cat Preston is the author of Murder in Menorca, the first book in the Abby Tennant cozy mystery series. With the first three books in the series being set on the beautiful island of Menorca, Abby Tennant is back at home in Book Four, in the picturesque South East of England.

Although Cat has spent the last twenty years in the project management sector, working mainly in London, since childhood she has always had dreams of being an author. Discovering cozy mysteries when she was first on maternity leave, Cat started writing her own stories a few years later. She loves writing stories about strong, independent women who juggle motherhood, work and life in general, celebrating all that women can achieve when they are surrounded by love and friendship.

Originally from Liverpool, Cat moved to the Garden of England with her young family, and has been there ever since. Cat likes nothing more than spending quality time with her boys, even if they don't feel the same way and have to be bribed away from their game consoles to get out in the English countryside.

Want to stay up to date? You can find Cat online at www.catprestonauthor.com. Subscribe to Cat's FREE monthly newsletter to keep up to date with new releases, giveaways and the occasional life in the countryside picture.

The next instalment of the Abby Tennant Mysteries is coming soon. In the meantime, if you want to catch up, here's some links to the earlier books:

UK Links:
Murder in Menorca: An Abby Tennant Mystery

Poolside: A Murder in Menorca Abby Tennant Mystery

Hidden Treasure: A Murder in Menorca Abby Tennant Mystery

Murder at the Fair: An Abby Tennant Mystery

Murder Woods: An Abby Tennant Mystery

US Links:
Murder in Menorca: An Abby Tennant Mystery

Poolside: A Murder in Menorca Abby Tennant Mystery

Hidden Treasure: A Murder in Menorca Abby Tennant Mystery

Murder at the Fair: An Abby Tennant Mystery

Murder Woods: An Abby Tennant Mystery

Printed in Great Britain
by Amazon

33670863R00110